AF432323

Ursa Major

Prologue

Tension filled the room like water fills a sponge, creating a certain atmosphere of thick suspense that engulfed the area like a blanket. Air heavy, hot and syrupy.

Nervously, Nicodemo closed the door of his childhood friend's flat behind him as gently as his shaking hands would let him. As he entered the flat he wondered to himself how he had managed to land himself in this mess, and whether it would be a better idea to turn around and go back home.

Instead of letting his nerves get the better of him, however, Nico swallowed the lump in his throat and raised his eyes to stare straight ahead to the open balcony doors across the room. The smog of the city drifted upwards to the heavens outside, but even being out in that grime and filth would make Nico more comfortable than he was now.

"I hope you brought the money..." came the menacing voice belonging to the silhouette on the balcony: the aforementioned childhood friend, "...For your own sake."

Feeling the thumping inside his chest, Nico took one tentative step forwards.

"That's just the thing," he started, breaths unsteady, "I don't have it yet."

There was silence as the air thickened further, choking him. The fumes outside made breathing difficult enough already, but this was just overkill.

"Then why are you here?"

As Nico approached a little further, he could see his friend in more detail. He was tall, blond and had a look on his face not unlike one an aggravated politician might bear.

"I need more *time,*" Nico begged him, "A month, maybe two, that's all! I promise I can have it by then!"

"That's what you said last time."

"This time it's true! I swear!"

"How do I know if you're lying to me?"

"I've never lied to you. Come on, we've been friends since before we could walk. I've never done anything to wrong you in my *life,*" Nico told him, solemnly, "And I never will, if I can help it."

Nervously, he stepped right in front of his friend, looking up ever so slightly to meet his eyes. Surely he could remember all their childhood years together, and the times they shared through their teens. A little disagreement over a loan between friends couldn't be the thing to break that bond…

"Nico, unlike you, I've worked years to be able to finally support myself. Not with a lot, but at least I have a house with heating. I'm not about to let you leech off me like this."

"I..."

Nico swallowed and it seemed to burn his throat on its way down. His pale skin felt clammy and his legs felt like they were about to snap off at the knees, sending the rest of his body to an impromptu meeting with the floor.

"Please, buddy, you've been such a good friend to me all these years, we aren't going to let a tiny loan spoil it all, are we?… Are we?"

He got his answer in the form of being grabbed by the collar and roughly pushed up against the filthy glass barrier of the balcony.

"If you don't have the money by tomorrow… you'll have another thing coming."

Nico tried to speak, to choke out a word or two, but no matter how hard he tried he couldn't make a sound. His vision blurred and pumped from fear and shock and his legs quivered even more.

He was then released with a hefty shove which normally would have left him nothing worse than dazed. This time however he realised something terrible was about to happen as he felt the glass of the balcony crack against his back.

The last thing Nico saw was the face of his childhood friend slip downwards in his vision, and his gaze met the sky, the smog and the glaring lights as the glass shattered behind him. His heart seemed to stay up there on the balcony while the rest of his body fell away like a brick for two storeys.

The last thing that his so-called 'buddy' saw as he stared down from the balcony was the inanimate form of his debtor laying lifeless on the ground alongside the remains of a perfectly innocent artificial plant that had joined him in his descent.

And the only thing that the liable creditor thought to do regarding this sight was to cover his mouth with a cold hand as realisation hit him, and to get away as fast as his legs would carry him.

<u>Chapter 1: Big Brother</u>

Barret Orson slowly fried two lonely eggs in a pan that was way too big for their size, in a manner that suggested he'd gone through the action so many times it had become automatic. He sighed and pulled a fed-up face as he stared, abstractedly, at the bubbling oil.

Like a dull drone in the background, the noises of the city outside sounded on for yet another morning. Engines growling by, people talking, yelling, babies crying, the clamour of the loud adverts ringing out their routine chimes, the rattling of the heavy rain upon the window pane. The name 'Eden' didn't suit the city at all, yet it was the name it bore nonetheless.

The year was 2084 and, frankly, Barret was shocked the world had survived this long. It shouldn't have, by any means, and everything was falling apart anyway, but here it was.

"EGGS!" Barret yelled across the room to the dark doorway at the other end. He took the pan off the heat and scraped the eggs onto two plates.

The apartment he resided in was cold, dark and grimy, yet this wasn't his fault. It was his parents' flat but presently they were both at work, and had been since five that morning. They wouldn't return home until late that night, either. This was how it was every day, but Barret stayed home; after all, somebody had to look after his little brother.

Rubbing his tired eyes with his fingers, Barret heard the familiar tentative footsteps of his brother, Ambrose, making his way out of the bedroom for breakfast. By the speed of his steps, he'd evidently only just woken up.

"Just us today, buddy," Barret said, fixing his brown curly hair.

"Again," Ambrose replied. He was only nine years old, and ever since he was a baby he hadn't ever seen much of his parents.

Money was tight. Too tight. It probably couldn't get any tighter. During the last six months, they'd had to sell the TV and one of the couches to try and raise enough money to buy food. The place only had three rooms and for a week now the family had been living off eggs and sardines.

"You said we could go to the cinema soon, Bear," Ambrose said as he began to eat his breakfast. He always called Barret 'Bear', due to his height, his muscular build and the fact that inside he had the personality of a big teddy bear.

"Well, I… I don't know, I might not have enough saved for that yet..."

"You *promised.*"

"I know I did. I know..." Barret sighed, leaning his elbows on the counter-top. He earned as much as he could by fixing electronics now and again, but he hadn't had any customers in a long time and it didn't pay so well anyway. He used every penny he earned trying to make Ambrose happy.

"You know what?" he started, decidedly, standing up straight at once, "Tomorrow, after dinner, I'll take you along to the cinema and we'll watch whatever you want."

"Really???" Ambrose grinned, ecstatically, almost choking on his breakfast.

"Yes, really."

"Thank you, Bear! You're the best big brother ever!"

Barret managed a weak smile before he drifted away into the bedroom that the four of them shared. It was a bare room, with only the four little beds, a sideboard, a clothes rack and a box of a few possessions they had, including a set of dumbbells. Barret kept his debit card secret so that his parents wouldn't find it and try to use it, and right now it was hidden on top of a broken air conditioning unit near the ceiling. Being the grand height of six foot five, Barret could reach it no problem, but nobody else could.

Before he left the room, he turned his attention to the tablet on the small wooden sideboard. It was the only piece of technology that hadn't yet been sold because Barret guarded it with a passion. It was his one window to the outside world – the world outside Eden City – and he wasn't about to let anybody sell it.

A notification from a news article flashed up on the screen, announcing that an escaped convict was currently roaming Eden, complete with mugshot.

Barret frowned. He hated stepping foot outside nowadays, never mind taking Ambrose. Every day the conditions of the city just kept falling further and further into darkness…

If there was one thing he wanted, it was to get out of this grimy flat, away from his parents, and make a difference… or just *get out* at all. See a nice tree or two perhaps.

What he didn't foresee, though, was how that would happen.

It thundered that night, and rained harder than it had ever rained before. The lightning was the one infrequent illumination throughout the apartment, and every time it struck, Ambrose would lean a little further into his brother's side.

"It's outside," Barret reminded him, kindly, "It can't hurt you."

He balanced his tablet on his knee. He'd been trying to distract his little brother with cartoons but so far they weren't doing a particularly good job. Every time there was a storm it would be like this.

"What about the thunder?" Ambrose trembled.

"Thunder isn't dangerous, it's just a sound the lightning makes to scare you."

Their conversation was interrupted by the noise of the front door opening and two individuals entering.

"Sounds like mum and dad are back, huh?" Barret hummed, leaving Ambrose with the tablet as he rose and went to say hello.

Barret's father had been as tall as a tree in his youth and surprisingly heavyset. Years of factory work had given him a hunchback and a bad temper. His ever-cross face was wrinkled from stress and his hair dulled into a dark grey.

His mother, on the other hand, was small and delicate, with hollow cheeks and thin lips, but still equally as ill-tempered. Her eyes had dark bags underneath and every sentence was plagued by a rattling smoker's cough. Life hadn't treated her well so far, and by the looks of things it was only heading downhill from here.

"Did you have a good day at work?" Barret started, cautiously, hoping he wouldn't spark an altercation.

"What do you think?" his father shot back, "Your mother and I spend all day every day working as hard as humanly possible just so we can scrape together enough money to pay the bills and when we come home, here you are, acting as if everything's fine. Maybe you had a good day, what did you do, hmm? Just sit around doing nothing?"

"I made eggs…"

"Your father and I have had a talk," his mother put in then, putting her hands on her hips, "And we've come to the conclusion that there's one too many mouths to feed in this house."

"Wh… What do you mean?"

"It means you're out, Barret," his father snapped, "You're twenty-six and it's about time you got out of here and made your own way in the world. Maybe it'll help you appreciate how hard it is to live in this society."

"You mean I have to move out? Where to?"

"You'll find somewhere. And you'll need a real job, too."

"But who's going to look after Ambrose?"

Barret ran his hands through his hair in a state of panicked disbelief. He'd been looking after Ambrose since his birth, it was the only reason he stuck around. He was the only one who really knew the boy and had his best interests at heart. He'd dedicated his young adulthood to being a good protector – Ambrose might not have even survived infancy if it weren't for him. He couldn't just leave now.

"He's old enough to look after himself."

"He's *nine!* That's hardly old enough to be left home alone, never mind cook for himself."

"You managed."

"I-" he stuttered, "I *shouldn't* have! It's a wonder I'm still here!"

"We've made our decision, Barret."

"You can't just kick me out like that! *Please!*"

"Pack your essentials and nothing but."

"I…"

"You're leaving in the morning."

Barret swallowed shakily and cast a gaze across to the bedroom doorway, where he saw the scared face of Ambrose peeking past the door. They made eye contact for a few seconds and both of them had an air of frightened helplessness. Barret made his way to the bedroom, feeling a bit dead, and gently pulled his brother back in by the shoulder.

"Come on, buddy," he sighed, "Why don't you come and help me pack?"

"What about the cinema, Bear?"

"We're still going, some day. I promised, didn't I?"

It was the next day that Barret found himself out on the streets of Eden with nothing but his small bag of possessions on his back and a saddened frown on his face. He didn't know why he hadn't expected it, his folks had been pushing him to get into factory work for months now.

He'd packed practically all he owned: his tablet, a couple of outfits, some smaller weights that weren't too heavy, his toothbrush and toothpaste, and a traditional style teddy bear – a gift from his late grandmother – he'd had since he was only a baby. It had been his faithful companion ever since. He'd almost left it with Ambrose but his little brother wanted him to keep it by his side.

Ambrose had cried his little heart out, of course, when Barret left. No number of assurances of 'I'll be back' could calm him, and his weeping had persisted until Barret was no longer in earshot.

His heart aching inside his chest, Barret tugged his hood over his head against the wind and the rain. Where did he go now? What would he do? All he could think about was his little brother missing him back home, though he knew he'd return eventually.

The clamour of the city filled his ears, but it all morphed into a dull drone, like a thick milkshake of noise. The rain poured on and Barret could feel his red nose and cheeks numbing in the biting September cold. The only thing he had on his side was his height and his build, which he hoped meant that it was less likely for somebody to pick a fight with him. From the outside, he must have looked rather intimidating, which he supposed was where he got his nickname. But this grizzly really was just a teddy on the inside.

Somebody knocked into his arm then as they ran past, and Barret stumbled to the side. He hadn't been paying attention to where he had been walking, as his mind was too distracted with thoughts of what he was leaving behind. His foot met a deep puddle and his sock soaked up an uncomfortable amount of water through the hole in his shoe.

Looking up, he was met with the sight of a poster pinned up on a lamp-post, an advertisement announcing that there was a vacancy in a flat nearby for a new occupant. A roof room, shared with two other people. Moving in with two strangers and adopting a new lifestyle might not be the best idea… and yet…

He took a note of the address and phone number before snaking off to find shelter.

Barret hadn't really expected the flat to be as nice as it was. It was large and airy, on the very top floor of an apartment block. Decorations, however, were minimal. The kitchenette was tiny, the couches looked like they had seen better days and the TV was probably older than Ambrose. The apartment itself, though, was a lot nicer than Barret's old home. Although that wasn't saying much. It was mostly open-plan, with floor to ceiling windows all on one side. The rooms were generously sized with slightly scratched white floors and shiny walls to match. A few of the walls had big, bright, modern stripes on them to add a pop of colour, and whatever decorations were around were brightly-coloured too.

One of the existing occupants showed him round, a man by the name of Marcus Morris. He was the same height as Barret, broad-shouldered, spoke with a pleasant Jamaican accent and was missing his little finger on his left hand. At first glance, he seemed a little intimidating, with the deep voice and the strong stature, but in all reality he was of exceedingly pleasant disposition.

They stopped at the sleeping quarters, containing four cheaply-made beds, two on each side of the room, pretty far apart with dividing half-walls between them, a bit like a more spacious hostel room. Everyone had their own space in here, despite it being one room. A hammock hung loosely from the roof beams at the end. It seemed a nice place and Marcus was friendly enough so Barret was strongly leaning towards the idea of staying.

"Do I get to meet the other... occupant?" He asked with a hint of nervousness. The butterflies in his stomach hadn't died down since he got here and they didn't feel like they were going to any time soon.

"Leyland? You'll meet him before you move in. He's an alright guy," Marcus assured him, but still, Barret couldn't help being uneasy.

This place was probably going to be his only option. Adapting to the lifestyle would be... interesting. But he supposed he'd just have to see how it goes. Rent was cheap enough, it got him off the streets and he got to meet new people who would hopefully help him out in his new life. Thoughtfully, he nodded and gazed around the long bedroom.

"When can I move in?"

Within the first month in his new home, Barret had learned a lot about his housemates and the life they lived. There was a place to climb up to the roof from the balcony beside the kitchenette and Barret liked to sit up there to think, but when he wasn't there, he took pleasure in people-watching.

His flatmates had asked if he had a nickname. Barret didn't really have a given nickname, but he supposed he could get used to 'Bear', which was of course what Ambrose used to call him. Everyone called him Bear now, and he'd started to like it so much he called himself by it too. Besides, if he was making a new start, why not have a new name? So Bear it was.

Leyland, the second of the housemates, spent most of his time outside. He went primarily by the nickname 'Spitfire' and everyone called him by it no matter how silly it sounded. He was athletic and sported a mess of blond hair in a punky cut that was dyed bright green at the tips. He was cool-headed and used a lot of incomprehensible slang to cover up his junior-grade vocabulary. Although not being the most friendly, he wasn't horrible either. This was of no consequence as he and 'Bear' didn't talk much.

These were Bear's observations over the past thirty days. He watched the other guys a lot as they did their own thing, but preferred not to 'hang out' with them. He'd fixed the TV on his second day and Marcus and Spitfire had been greatly impressed. On his third day he trained with the workout equipment that was already in the flat for eight hours straight. The running machine was a bit old but it worked and it was a lot better than the dumbbells that he'd had at home. Bear had placed the weights he'd brought with him in the 'exercise corner' and now they were for anyone's use. When money was this tight, sharing was always a good idea.

Except maybe in the case of toothbrushes. There's always exceptions.

So now, in his second month here, Bear busied himself running on the treadmill and keeping himself in shape. He'd always been one to keep fit, not wanting to end up like his father, and reasoning that it was probably a good idea to be strong enough to defend yourself if you lived in a place like Eden.

He was home alone, as the others had gone out to work. Marcus was a self defence teacher and Spitfire worked delivering fast food (he didn't seem to enjoy it so he never spoke of it, always seemed to be frustrated by the amount of money he made. Or didn't make).

So there was Bear, with a worn towel around his neck, treadmill set to hill climb, panting as he kept a steady pace. Two wireless earbuds sat comfortably in his ears, playing some alternative rock as he ran. He enjoyed being alone in the flat, as amicable as his housemates were.

But whenever he was alone, Bear couldn't help thinking about Ambrose. Poor, lost Ambrose… How was he going to manage without his big brother there to protect him? How lonely it was going to be at home... The family hadn't ever been able to afford to send him to school so he spent every day at home. Now he'd be on his own in a dark, cold flat… Sometimes Bear took his secret Teddy out of his bag and stared into its deep brown eyes and thought all about his little brother at home.

Scared.

Alone.

Interrupting his day like an unexpected fire drill, a violent clatter sounded from the next room. The kind of noise you'd hear if you were to drop a large dog onto a set dinner table.

With a stumble, Bear slowed down the treadmill to a stop and removed his earbuds. He narrowed his eyes and listened carefully for any other noise, of which there was none. Tensing, he pulled the towel off his shoulders and held it taut in his strong hands. What a towel could do to protect him against a potential intruder he did not know but he took it anyway. Carefully, he crept towards the doorway and slowly craned his neck around to see what was going on.

There, in a tangled mess, upside down against a couch opposite the open window, was the form of a figure. A long cable snaked across the floor from their hand to the window.

Bear made eye contact and the figure let out a quivering shriek.

Chapter 3: Spider

Bear stumbled backwards to the open window, yelling in panic and confusion.

"WHO ARE YOU???" He yelped, clutching his trusty towel as threateningly as he could.

The figure stared back to him in terror and hurriedly struggled to right himself,

"WHO ARE *YOU*?" He retorted to Bear, gathering together the cord that was strung all the way across the floor. It looked to come from a silver box-like thing strapped to his right arm. On the end of it, near the window, was a grappling hook.

"What do you mean 'who are you'? I live here!" Bear snapped back, waving his hands about in confusion.

"Not last week!"

"And how would you know? Do you fly through people's windows often?"

The figure scrambled to his feet and Bear could get a better look at him.

He wore a long, burgundy, skin-tight hoodie with spider webs sewn onto the shoulders, a red mask over his mouth and nose, a pair of what Bear could only assume were a type of running trouser, and a thick utility belt around the hips.

Overall, his vibe was oddly cartoonish and non-human.

Bear placed his fingers on his temples and rubbed them as he heaved a sigh.

"OK, let's start from the top," he muttered, "What's your name?"

"Spider," the visitor said, stepping forward, the grappling hook trailing behind him.

Bear looked down to him (quite a way, too: Spider could only have been about five foot four). Yeah, he *did* look like a spider. Bear held out a hand,

"I'm Bear," he said as Spider took his hand in a manner that suggested he hadn't shaken many hands in his lifetime. He had long, flimsy fingers that wrapped weakly around Bear's large palm, "What brings you… to my flat?"

"...Dropping in..." Spider replied. His voice was somewhat scratchy yet not in an annoying way and he rolled his 'R's in a sort of strange purr.

Usually, Bear could read people like a book. When he met Marcus, he could tell that he was genuine. When he met Spitfire, he could tell he had a limited vocabulary just by looking at him move for a bit. But with this 'Spider' guy, the pages were closed tight; for whatever reason, Bear just couldn't figure out what kind of a person he was. He seemed, on first glance, like a dark and mysterious individual, but when he opened his mouth, he sounded rushed and a bit unhinged.

Bear dropped his hand and wiped his palm on the towel.

"You said I didn't live here last week," he started, "Do you… *drop in* a lot?"

Spider gathered together the cord from the grappling hook in his hands and started to feed it back into the box-like device on his arm. The hook itself folded into a bullet shape that fit snugly into the end of the container.

"Sometimes," he replied, shortly.

"You know Marcus and the others?"

"Acquaintances."

"For how long?"

"A year? Three?"

"You're not friends, then?"

"Cordial."

"And you come… smashing through the windows every time?"

"That bit was an accident."

Spider brushed himself down and snaked off over to the fridge, which he then opened and stuck his head into. He frowned at the lack of snacks contained within it and shut the door with visible irritation. He then ran the tap, pulled his mask down and twisted his head so he could drink. There was a cup beside the sink but he clearly didn't care to use it.

"Anything I can... get you?" Bear offered, awkwardly. He made eye contact with Spider as he turned around and neither of them spoke.

Spider's appearance at that moment was surely something. Water dripped steadily down his pointy chin but he attempted to lick it off, still maintaining eye contact. His teeth were sharp, canines practically catlike fangs, and his eyes glinted with a mischievous spark.

"No," he replied, "Ta."

"Were you looking for somebody?"

"Marcus. Need a favour."

"What kind of a favour? Maybe I can help you out," Bear suggested, leaning over to right all the things that Spider had knocked over when he had made his colourful entrance.

"It's nothing," Spider shrugged, running his tongue around his mouth thoughtfully as he leaned back on the counter-top, dangerously close to the glass.

At the sound of a door unlocking from behind, his ears metaphorically pricked up.

"Somebody's home," he chirruped, stating the obvious.

There was a short staircase down to the front door and soon footsteps could be heard climbing it. Fairly light footsteps at that, so it couldn't be Marcus.

Sure enough, moments later, Spitfire appeared at the top of the stairs. His eyes met Spider's immediately and the look on his face was not one of excitement in the slightest. Flicking a glance to Bear, he heaved a sigh.

"I see you've met Spider," he said. Clearly he'd had the pleasure of meeting this... *interesting* character before.

"Yeah, he was just saying you'd all met before, I..." Bear started, but when he turned to gesture to his new acquaintance, Spider had simply disappeared, leaving not a trace of his presence but a wobbling glass, which then unceremoniously toppled over.

"He does that," Spitfire said.

Bear blinked once, slowly, wondering whether that whole encounter had just happened or if he was simply beginning to lose his marbles. Then he blinked again.

"Does he come around here a lot?"

"Pretty much all the time, which is too much for my liking," Spitfire frowned, obviously not fond of Spider, "He pops in with no warning, sticks around for less than a day, takes all the good snacks and leaves again."

Bear wondered why Spider hadn't been mentioned to him before, but from the look on Spitfire's face, he could tell that he wasn't a very popular character...

Maybe with some digging, Bear could figure out *why*... and just exactly *who* this enigmatic individual was...

<u>Chapter 4: Arachnophobia</u>

The sunlight shimmered in cosy, warm beams through the window and stretched out over the bedroom floor in pools of gold. A flurry of flecks of dust from the old furniture drifted through the air, showing up in the light, making the usually hidden scruffiness of the apartment even more evident.

The blinds over the window broke up the beams in a shutter-like pattern, making the flooring look a bit like a zebra crossing.

On this fine morning, Bear wasn't so bothered about taking in the sunlight or enjoying the early morning vibe; he was too busy sat on his mattress, holding the old traditional teddy in front of his face. He was thinking about Ambrose, or at least trying to.

There came a gentle clatter and a bubbling from the kitchenette in the next room, as the old coffee machine stirred to life with a clunk. Clearly, somebody was starting the day off with a hot shot of caffeine. Probably Marcus, as Spitfire usually favoured some energy drink or other. Bear wasn't in the mood for either.

As the traffic whooshed past outside and the aroma of espresso drifted through the air, Bear did nothing but stare into the little teddy's eyes and wonder.

He was beginning to formulate a little plan in his mind. He knew he had to get Ambrose out of that house somehow; there was no way he'd be happy and cared-for back there. The first step, however, would be pooling together enough money to get into a more comfortable living situation, then go on an Ambrose rescue mission.

Thinking about how nice it would be to live alone with his little brother in an apartment all of their own… it made Bear's heart warm slightly. He hugged the teddy to his chest and laid back down on his bed. Even though this thought made him happy, his mind still kept wandering back to Spider, that puzzling character he'd met yesterday.

His movements, the way he spoke… it was almost inhuman in a way. He was clearly very streetwise and experienced with his grappling hook, or he would have been dead long ago. But perhaps the most perplexing thing about him was the fact that Bear could read nothing into his personality. He couldn't tell if Spider was a good person, a bad person, dangerous or innocent… and maybe that was why he was so interesting. Magnetic, almost. But Bear didn't *want* to think about Spider – he rather wished he'd get out of his head like he disappeared out of the window yesterday – he didn't want *anything* to distract him from his objective of rescuing his little brother.

Hearing footsteps approaching, Bear stuffed the teddy back under the bunk and sat up straight, going light-headed for a few seconds from the sudden movement.

Soon, Marcus' face appeared, looking over the short room divider.

"We need some errands running today," he said, in his regular flat tone.

As much as Bear hated going back on the streets, he was the only one available today to do these jobs, and if he didn't do them, he'd no doubt lose favour with his flatmates.

"What kind of errands?" he asked, stretching out his stiff arms.

"Getting food, mostly," Marcus replied, "I wrote a list."

He handed Bear a short list of food items and other things to search for (short, because that was all they could really afford) and slowly sipped coffee out of his chipped mug.

"I'll see what I can do," Bear replied, and received a thumbs-up of thanks in return. He got to his feet and looked about for his shoes and a bag. Looking on the bright side, maybe going down into the belly of the city would help take his mind off Spider…

Sirens and shouting filled the air, accompanied occasionally by the blaring noise of an advertisement on some billboard announcing offers on the latest technology and fashions (adverts for people with more money than Bear, that was for sure). There was a strong stench drifting through the streets, like a bitter and pungent mix of tobacco smoke and grease from the run-down takeaways lining the alleys. It smelled like diseases, of which people around this part of the city had quite the collection.

It had become customary for people to wear surgical masks when down here, to stop themselves adding to their personal accumulation of ailments. If you bravely ventured even further into the stomach of Eden, you would reach the roughest zone of all, where surgical masks were replaced with gas masks to provide some meagre protection against the fumes and pollution spilling out from the nearby factory.

On the other end of the spectrum, the outskirts of the city were actually rather pleasant and clean. They were the glossy magazine cover that hid the filth underneath, and were properly referred to as the Magenta District.

Bear never went to the Magenta District; the people there could tell he came from the harsher parts, and weren't afraid to show it in their condescending glares. Besides, any shop over there selling anything worth buying would be well out of Bear's price range, so he stuck to the slums.

Currently, the rain was just beginning to drip, as if the sky was spitting on the city in disgust.

Bear pulled his hood up over his head and fixed the mask over his mouth as he regarded the list Marcus had provided him with. The first item on it was fish. People such as Marcus, Bear and the others practically lived on protein.

So, keeping a tight grip on the paper, Bear made his way through the narrow streets to the little fishmonger's, a dark and cold shop that contributed a large extent towards the foul smell.

The fishmonger's name was Torsten Frangleton, which Bear regarded as a wildly unfortunate name before realising that he shared a home with someone who called himself by the name of a plane.

Bear asked politely for a selection of the cheapest fish available and, after receiving his order, paid up with crumpled notes and stuffed the seafood in his brown satchel. He then locked the padlock over the buckle (you never could take too many precautions around these parts), thanked Torsten and left.

He was quite fortunate in the fact that nobody had ever picked a fight with him, probably due to his impressive stature, but he still stepped carefully.

Leaving the shop, he was sure he caught a glimpse of sudden movement from the corner of his eye. The streets were mildly crowded today so it may very well have been nothing, but the fact that Bear specifically noticed it made it seem a touch suspicious.

Regarding it as nothing, he moved on, but every half a minute or so it appeared again, almost as if following him. Still, Bear tried to ignore it, just kept his fingers wrapped tightly around the strap of his satchel.

Checking the list again, he saw that the next thing he had to find was soap. Carbolic, probably, whatever was cheap. Most of the household funds went into paying the rent, so they tried to save as much as they possibly could on everything else.

As he walked, the elusive shadow kept flickering past in the corner of Bear's eye. His first tactic of ignoring it clearly wasn't working, so when he felt it behind him he stopped in his tracks in the middle of a mostly-empty street and sighed.

"Are you tailing me?" he asked without turning around, hoping that anyone watching wouldn't think he'd gone crazy.

"Would you like me to stop?" came the voice from behind, and Bear's heart dropped like a brick inside his chest as he immediately recognised it.

Turning around, he looked down to find himself facing the small figure of Spider.

"I'd like you to tell me why," he frowned. He had really been hoping that yesterday would be the last he ever saw of Spider.

"Guilt," Spider replied, hanging his head, showing that his hood had about six spider eyes embroidered into it. His long, wild, black hair flopped down over his face a bit, weighed down by the hood and the rain, and his sharp eyes flicked up from the wet ground to look up at Bear like a sad puppy.

"Guilt?"

"I scared you yesterday."

"So you thought that following me would make up for it?"

"I wanted to apologise."

"You could have just walked up to me, you know?"

Spider shrugged.

"Nervous," he said.

"Do you do this to a lot of people?"

"Not as yet. Should I?"

"No, please don't," Bear told him, then rubbed his temples, "Look, Spider… If I forgive you for flying through my window, will you leave me alone?"

"Okay."

But before Bear could utter the words 'I forgive you for flying through my window', he felt a tug on his shoulder as his satchel was ripped from him.

"HEY!" he shouted after the figure now disappearing with it. It was the only thing he could think to do in his mildly stunned state.

Before he could go after the thief, Spider shot out after the figure like an arrow straight from the bow of a master archer, moving in and out between unknowing citizens like a snake as he kept hot on the tail of the crook. Within seconds, he had disappeared down a back alley.

Bear stood, still stupefied. Did Spider just team up with a thief to distract him so that he could pinch his satchel and hightail it? In all honesty, he wouldn't be surprised.

What would Marcus do if he returned home not only without provisions but also without the money and the bag? Bear didn't wish to think about it. He only stared down the street to where Spider had disappeared and willed the ground to cave in beneath him.

To his relief, however, Spider soon reappeared… with a bag swung over his shoulder.

He merrily trotted towards Bear like a dog having successfully recovered the ball its owner had thrown, and stopped right in front of him, presenting him with the satchel.

"Here you go," he said, in a rather casual voice that made it sound as if this was a thing that happened quite often.

"Th... Thank you," Bear responded, shortly, gently taking the bag.

"You're welcome."

Spider brushed himself down and cleared his throat.

"I'll be going, then," he announced, abruptly, "See you around," and he turned to leave.

"Wait, wait, Spider-" Bear started, reaching out to take him by the shoulder, "Why don't you... come with me for a bit? If you're not busy."

"Really???" Spider chirruped, his eyes lighting up as he turned around.

"Yeah, sure," Bear nodded.

"But wait... Do you forgive me for the window?" Spider asked, concerned suddenly.

"Yes, I forgive you for the window," Bear chuckled lightly, "Come on, let's go."

Seated on the couch with a cardboard cup of budget instant coffee in his hands, Bear looked across to his new friend.

Spider was busy cleaning his grappling hook and checking it over for any faults in the wire. He had positioned himself on the end of one of the dividing half-walls (he had a tendency to choose the strangest places to sit) and was perched there neatly.

It had been a good five hours since they'd met down on the street and Bear had talked and rambled for the grand majority of that time. What Spider didn't know about him at this point, he didn't even know himself. Spider just had such a quiet disposition, a listening look upon his face, and Bear had found himself pouring out his life story to him. All about his parents, his home, about Ambrose… and Spider had listened intently all the way through, hardly speaking a word.

Now they were both back at the flat, as the rain carried on drizzling outside.

"I don't know why I've told you all this," Bear sighed, swirling what was left of his drink around in his cup, "You know all about me but I don't know anything about you…"

"There's not much to say," Spider replied, without making eye contact.

"Well, where do you live? That's a start."

"I have places."

"You… 'have places'?"

Spider nodded.

Bear had a feeling that this question was not going to be answered in any more detail.

"Alright, so, what was your childhood like?" he asked instead.

"'Dunno."

"How about your name? Your real name? You know mine already."

Spider finally looked down to him, a blank look upon his face, and shrugged.

"You don't need to know about me."

"But I'd like to," Bear told him, leaning forwards so that his elbows were resting on his knees. He received no response, as Spider only shook his head and returned his attention to his grappling hook, gathering the wire together in his hands.

"Sorry," he said.

Bear sighed again,

"Don't worry about it. I won't push you."

Spider's reluctance to reveal anything about himself was only heightening Bear's curiosity. Still, he didn't wish to seem overly nosy. Gaining Spider's trust was the first step to finding out who he really was, and it seemed that it was going to take a lot longer than first expected.

Bear rose from the sofa, draining his cup and tossing it into the bin in the corner of the room. His eyes drifted up to the window and watched, for a second or two, the raindrops against the glass.

"Pretty wet out there," he noted, stating the obvious, "Not the best weather for walking home, huh?"

"I've been out in the dark with the rain before. Many times."

"I thought maybe you'd like to stick around here for a while longer. You're good company. More interesting than my flatmates, that's for sure."

"They don't like me much," Spider stated, tossing the grappling hook onto the bed beside him. He shuffled around a bit on the wall, making himself comfy.

Bear turned to him, gazing across with a sympathetic air.

"Really? Why?" he inquired.

Spider threw his head back in a loud cackle, clearly rather amused by the question. Every so often he'd do something or move a certain way and his whole look would be suddenly and uncomfortably uncanny.

"I'm a *creep*..." he purred, rolling the 'R', as he eased out of his laugh and returned to his usual posture. He retained a smirk as he met Bear's gaze.

"I… I wouldn't go *that* far..."

"*Rrrr*eally, now, Bear… You've met me…"

"It doesn't *feel* like I've met you," Bear replied, heaving a breath and slowly shaking his head.

"Hey, me neither," Spider shrugged, dropping down from the half-wall and assessing whether it really was too wet to go back out again.

Bear did not know what he meant by what he said, but didn't press another question.

"You know what? Maybe I will stay a little longer. You're good company, too," Spider smiled, "I think we're gonna get along just *fine...*"

"Customer assistant… nah… Warehouse operative… definitely not..."

Bear sighed and scrolled downwards on his tablet screen once more. He regarded the job listing of 'bar staff' with visible contemplation before swiftly dismissing this one, too. As he reached the end of the final page, Bear let out a groan and laid back down on his mattress with a heavy *'thwump'*.

He'd never be able to get his own place if he didn't get a job. And he'd never be able to save Ambrose from that grimy flat with his parents if he didn't get his own place. But no matter how hard he looked, none of the jobs he found appealed to him. They were either too monotonous, or the wrong environment, or in the wrong part of Eden. Back at home, he'd made his money by fixing computers and other devices, but since his move, he hadn't had any business.

He sat up once more and knelt just high enough to peer over the dividing wall to where Spider was at rest in the hammock at the end of the room, still dressed in his clothes from the day behind them. Bear wondered what he was dreaming about.

Quickly, Spider opened his eyes to stare back at him, as if he knew he was being watched.

Bear's eyes widened in a surprised guilt, but neither he nor Spider broke the unblinking gaze. Awkwardly, trying not to wake Marcus, who was asleep in the bed opposite him, Bear spoke up.

"Did I wake you?" he whispered.

Spider shook his head, trying to sit himself up, his fingers clumsily getting caught up in the rope as he did so.

"What was the groan for?"

"Oh, nothing, I'm just… job searching."

"Why?"

"Well, I need money if I'm going to try and buy my own flat, don't I?"

"You fix things."

"Yeah, but nobody has given me anything to fix recently. I'm penniless."

Spider gave a thoughtful squint, his eye glinting in the beam of street-light seeping in through the gap in the curtains, and then promptly turned over and went to sleep. This was not much help.

Bear had no idea if Spider had taken in any information from their discussion, whether his eyes had been sympathetic or indifferent, and, upon a bit of further reflection, whether the conversation had really happened at all. Just as he was about to lie down and finally get some rest, the sound of a door locking from the next room echoed through the flat. Spitfire, clearly, who had gone out earlier to visit a friend in the dark.

Not really wanting to speak to him, Bear settled down under his thin blanket and closed his eyes, listening to Spitfire wander around the kitchen, open the fridge, shut it roughly and enter the sleeping quarters.

"What's the weirdo doing here?" he said, in an uncomfortably loud voice.

Bear's eyes snapped open and darted straight up to his housemate.

"Who, Spider?"

"Who else?"

"You really don't like him, do you?"

Spitfire stared down to Bear and raised his eyebrows as if to say 'and you *do?*'

"Listen, Bear, I like to think I'm the best athlete in this part of Eden, if not the whole of it," he frowned, gesturing to himself, sharply, "And *this guy* thinks he can drop in and outshine me just like that. Him and his stupid laugh..." and he spit a piece of chewing gum an impressive distance into the bin.

"I beg your pardon?"

"Have you seen that guy move? He goes over the roofs instead of on the ground."

Spitfire proceeded to move his hands in what could only be described as freestyle sign language, accompanied by some utterances of *'whoosh'* and *'nyoom'*.

"Bear, he's cuckoo."

Bear nodded slowly in understanding as Spitfire twirled his finger around at the side of his head to emphasize his point.

"I'm telling you, man, stay away from him. He's bad news. The freak..."

Bear swallowed a lump slowly making a home in his throat and nodded once more. It was at this moment that he realised what exactly he had done: he'd become accidentally involved with some fast-talking, curious stranger, shared his life story with him and now invited him into his home.

Now, what had he got himself into?

<u>Chapter 6: Up On the Roof</u>

There were many things that Bear had come to expect each day when he woke up. He knew that as soon as he became conscious he would hear the clattering of traffic from outside, people yelling and commonly the splashing of rain. He also knew that his flatmates would either be grumpy or not at home at all. A common sound that determined whether the apartment was empty or not was the grinding of the coffee machine trying to read the coffee pod code, as if it was a far-sighted grandfather attempting to decipher some small text. Spider was nowhere to be found, despite being here last night, but that was hardly shocking.

What Bear did not expect, however, was for his mid-morning reading (a book of unsolved mysteries) to be interrupted by a polite knock at the door. Visitors here were about as common as a day without somebody outside shrieking at the top of their lungs.

Bear cautiously put his book on the floor and made his way to the door at such a lacklustre rate it was shocking that the person knocking hadn't left by the time he got there.

"Hello?"

"Hey," replied a mildly nervous-looking teen with a laptop under his arm, "Are you, uhh… Are you the dude who does repairs?"

"Yeah. Yeah, that's me," Bear nodded, though he was slightly confused. Usually, potential customers would message him first before bringing him a faulty device. In fact, his address wasn't listed anywhere to his knowledge – he only gave it out to customers who had contacted him. Never mind, though, he wasn't about to turn down business when it came knocking at his door.

"Great! My laptop has been making this grinding noise lately, it sounds like *GHRRRRGRRRRRRRNHHHH*. Think you could take a look at that?"

"Sure, leave it with me until Friday and I'll see what I can do," Bear nodded, despite being slightly thrown by the unexpected computer impression.

"Man, thanks a lot, dude, I really appreciate it. It's a vintage though, so, be careful," the teen thanked him, placing in Bear's hands the, surprisingly heavy, large, clunky computer. He left with a wave, without even asking about prices, and presumably headed for college or the nearest coffee shop.

Bear retreated back inside the silent flat, settling down on the sofa to have a look at what his new job would entail. As per usual, however, his mind was distracted by wondering how the lad at his door had obtained this address. Couldn't be his parents' doing, as they didn't even know where he lived. Maybe one of his housemates… but they didn't seem like the type of people to want strangers at their door.

In any case, it was more than a little strange, but if it would help spread the word and build his business, Bear wasn't complaining.

As the evening chill set in and the sky started to darken, Bear set down his empty plate onto the kitchen sideboard and gazed out of the window. His flatmates were home for once, though as usual none of them were talking to him.

Silently, Bear slid open the glass door set between the two full-length windows and stepped out onto the tiny balcony. From here, he could see out over the city, and he usually would have seated himself down on the white plastic chair beside him, but today he turned to the steel ladder to his left and began to climb. The ladder led up to the flat roof of the building, where the noise of the city seemed distant and the view was astonishingly expansive.

Bear sat down a safe distance from the edge, as there was only a very short border to prevent him falling off the side of the building, and he leaned back on his hands. The building was in a sort of circle of shorter towers walled in by more lofty ones. Way down below, the colours were a dull mix of browns and muted yellows, but in the horizon were the pink and purple lights of the Magenta

District. Every so often, the thrumming of a helicopter would pass overhead, or a loud siren from down on the ground, but Bear took no note of the noises.

He often wondered what his life would be like if he had been born over in the more pleasant zones. Would his parents still have struggled with money? Would he still have had to take care of Ambrose? Would he have been living on his own sooner? Would he look down on the unfortunate people who resided in the undesirable area? Was it really better to grow up on the outskirts, or had living in the dumps taught him a thing or two? Did he even really want to know?

Behind him came running footsteps, scampering, that abruptly halted before turning into a tentative-footed walk.

"Spider," Bear said, without turning about.

"Bear," came Spider's voice, "How did you know it was me?"

"I had a feeling you'd turn up," Bear replied, finally moving his head to look up to the figure behind him. He reached into his hoodie's front pocket and pulled out a cereal bar of some description, "I even brought you a snack… You don't have a peanut allergy, do you?"

Spider sat down cross-legged beside him and took the bar from his large hand.

"Let's find out!" he smiled, unwrapping it.

"Where did you go last night?"

"Hmm?"

"You were asleep when I went to bed, and when I woke up this morning you weren't there."

"I left."

This was not quite the answer Bear was hoping for.

"…Is there a reason you don't stick around a lot?"

"Spitfire."

"You two don't get along, huh?"

Spider looked him in the eye with a contemplating stare, as if wondering whether elaborating would be worth it.

"When I see him… and he looks back at me..." here he paused to squint, "There's a familiarity I can't put my finger on. Like I've done something wrong. He hasn't forgiven me for it, whatever it was, if I even did anything at all."

This was probably the longest Spider had spoken in one go. He casually brushed off this whole thing within the space of two seconds and went back to his snack.

Bear pursed his lips in thought, contemplating the information he'd just been given. He had to admit, in the few times he'd seen Spitfire and Spider interact, there seemed to be something like an unspoken rivalry between them. He assumed it was due to what Spitfire said about Spider being able to manoeuvre across the rooftops like he did. Jealousy.

"So… you've met him before?" He began.

Spider shrugged, which only confused Bear further. For a good while, he said nothing, but then he finally remembered what had been on his mind all day.

"Spider… Did you give out my address?"

"Why?"

"Someone turned up at my door this morning and asked me to fix his laptop. Is he one of your buddies?"

"I put up a poster," Spider replied, simply, dislodging a single oat from his gum as he spoke, "...Or two…"

"Why?"

"It's your job. You want to move out, don't you? Save your brother?"

"Well… yeah..."

"When you talked about your brother, I could tell. You really want to get him out of that tiny flat. I thought I was helping..." he stopped mid-sentence and his sharp eyes grew a little wider in fear, "You're not mad, are you?"

Bear shook his head with a small smile,

"No. I'm not mad," he replied, kindly, "You're really interested in helping me and Ambrose?"

"I guess I am."

"I hear you're pretty good at… *parkour?*"

"So-so."

"If you wanted to help me out… I think we could make a pretty good team…"

"Spider is going to help me with my Ambrose 'rescue mission'. Isn't that great?"

"You're teaming up with… Spider?"

"Yeah. He seems really interested in helping me. Why?"

"I just wondered why you decided to trust him."

"Why not?"

Marcus gave a short, amused snort.

"On your head be it, man," he said, giving Bear a funny look before leaving him be.

Bear took this encounter with a pinch of salt. Admittedly, he was wary about trusting Spider himself, but he'd take all the help he could get. Besides, there was no rule saying he had to *stay* in association with Spider after the job was done…

He looked back down to the plans laid out in front of him, his genius strategy to get his little brother out of the scruffy flat and away from his cruel parents.

First he would wait until his parents were both out of the apartment. They worked almost all day every day, so that part wouldn't be difficult. Because there was no exterior staircase, and the only way into the flat was from the lobby of the building, Spider would have to traverse the rooftops and clamber down the side of the building until he reached Ambrose's window. He'd knock on the glass to alert Ambrose and when the window was open he would ask him to buzz Bear into the building. Thereafter, Bear could quickly help Ambrose get his things together and all three of them would disappear into the city. Simple enough.

Hopefully, Bear's parents would never track them down, and Bear and Ambrose could be happy living on their own in their nice airy apartment with neither mother nor father to hold them back. Maybe if he got a good enough job, Bear could afford to send Ambrose to school…

He gave a content smile, hoping deeply that his plan would work out. All he wanted was to have his little brother by his side –

his cub, if you will – and to finally live in a measure of peace. Maybe life wouldn't feel so harsh then. Maybe the city wouldn't feel so bad. A little partnership, a friendship... that would lighten his world.

The light tapping of Spider's footsteps upon the cold floor was what came next, and he appeared in front of the table moments later, looking down at Bear and his papers.

"Action plan?"

"Yes, Spider," Bear nodded, confidently, "This is it! Have a read over and see what you think."

Spider leaned over, reading upside-down, and scanned over the papers in the space of a minute. He had a thoughtful look on his face, contemplating the plan with clear interest.

"I like it!" he grinned, eventually, and Bear breathed a sigh of relief, "I only have one question."

Nervously, Bear signalled for him to continue.

"What are you waiting for?"

"...Pardon?"

"Seems to me like the sooner we get your little brother out of there the better. Saving up to buy a flat… that takes a while. Little Ambrose might not be so little by that time."

"So what you're saying is…?"

"Hey, why wait? Wouldn't living here be better than back there?"

Bear contemplated this for a good moment. His flatmates seemed pretty safe and trustworthy people. They weren't violent and didn't partake in any questionable practices; at least that he knew of. Maybe bringing Ambrose here wouldn't be a terrible idea… at least just until they could get their own place… It was warm here, they had food, and Bear was home most of the time so Ambrose would never be alone with the others anyway.

"You know what? Sure," Bear nodded, "The day after tomorrow."

"Really?" Spider asked, looking a touch surprised at this sudden decision.

Bear nodded again, firmly, resolute, and Spider broke out into a grin,

"Ye-*heah!*" he beamed, "Let's go for it!"

Bear couldn't help but smile back at his enthusiasm. He knew he'd made the right choice in trusting the elusive visitor. For now at least.

And so the day rolled around; a Monday, when both of Bear's parents would definitely be at work. It was mid-day, and both Bear and Spider stood at the bottom of the tall, creaky and worn apartment building. It wasn't a pleasant sight. The glass of each of the balconies was green-y grey and streaky, if in one piece at all. Wires stretched overhead like sticky drool from the gaping mouth of some bedraggled beast and vents on the walls puffed out steam from the few homes with heating.

Bear's parents' flat was about half way up the building. The bedroom window faced forwards onto the street so that Bear and Spider could see it from where they stood. It was darkened at the moment, probably to save electricity. Hopefully if Ambrose was home he'd be in the bedroom, reading, and would see Spider at the window.

"Ready, Spider?" Bear asked, turning to his right to look down to him. But Spider was nowhere to be seen.

Spinning about in a slight bit of panic, Bear scanned the area for the small figure. His ears were alerted to a clattering to the side and his eyes darted towards the source immediately to discover Spider leaned over with his arms inside a large bin.

"What are you doing???"

"Look what I found!" Spider chirped, knocking his head on the lid of the bin as he backed out and held up a watch, proudly, in his hands. It was gold-coloured and shone in the dim lighting, and *just might* have been stolen.

"That's great, pal, but we have a job to do, remember?"

Spider scuttled over to his side, dropping the watch, clearly deciding it wasn't worth keeping.

Bear slipped an arm around his shoulders and bent down slightly to point to the bedroom window.

"Can you get up there?" he asked, and Spider looked to evaluate the matter for a few seconds before giving a firm nod of affirmation, "Great! Go for it, bud," Bear grinned.

Spider returned the grin in his usually manic manner, quickly scanned the area and found himself a route up to the balcony. He crossed over the street to where the large bin stood and clambered up on top of it. There was a sort of small grate just above head height a way along the wall. It stuck out about a foot from the wall and supported a small tangle of cables. It didn't look as if it could support much weight but Spider took a chance and sprung up to it like a streetwise cat, pulling himself up so he could crouch and keep his balance.

Bear watched in a mix of admiration and curiosity as Spider continued to scale the building, using various ledges, fans and grates as steps to launch his small body onto. When at an appropriate height, he shot a glance over to the apartment building and stood up straight. He raised his arm up to eye-height and placed his other hand over the grappling hook box strapped to his wrist.

The bullet-shape shot out like an arrow, the metal prongs unfolding in the blink of an eye, and flew up to the balcony above Ambrose's window, where it clung snugly to the barrier. After giving the wire a sharp tug, Spider hopped off the ledge he was positioned on and swung elegantly to the other building like a sugar glider, where he dropped down to his feet safely on Ambrose's balcony.

Bear stared up, impressed greatly, and returned the thumbs-up that Spider gave him, although he wished he'd just get on with it.

Spider inelegantly pressed his face up against the window and peered inside. Almost immediately, though, a frown crossed his face.

"Are you sure this is the right flat?" he called.

"Yeah, one-hundred percent," Bear replied, confidently.

Spider squinted through the darkened window into the bedroom on the other side and tapped one of his long fingers on the glass.

"Yeah, OK, Bear, we have a problem."

Suddenly met with concern, a biting sensation started to gnaw at the pit of Bear's stomach. The foul stench in the air became overwhelmingly evident and his heart seemed to fall a few inches further into his chest.

"Wh- what's wrong?"

"It's empty, Bear."

"What do you mean it's empty?"

"I mean it's *empty!*" Spider retorted, leaning over the balcony railing and making a wildly enthusiastic hand gesture, "No lights on, no furniture, no sign of movement."

"No furniture? You mean, none at all?"

"Correct."

Bear stared up to him, a panic filling his heart. *That couldn't be right...*

"Are you sure there's nobody home? Try tapping on the window!"

"Okay... *As if that's going to bring back the furniture.*"

Spider did as he was told, giving the glass a few sharp taps with his finger. But after waiting a while, still nobody appeared inside. Even after a couple more rounds of knocking, there was no movement.

"Well maybe your folks took him out somewhere," Spider suggested, sensing Bear's worry.

"No, they couldn't, they work every Monday," Bear shot back, beginning to walk around in circles, clearly agitated. Even if they hadn't been at work, his parents weren't the kind to take their young son on a nice family day out.

Spider went back to pressing his nose to the glass and trying in vain to detect a sign of life inside. From the look on his face, he was feeling a good measure of concern about Ambrose, despite never having met him. After a minute or two of uncomfortable silence, bar the sounds of the downtrodden city, Spider brought up the fact that one of the neighbours may have heard or seen something that would give a pointer to where the Orson family would be.

The two stuck around the building a while longer, Bear deciding that asking a neighbour if they'd seen anything was probably the only way to locate his brother. Still, his heart raced. *What if they'd all moved away from him? What if they were... no, he didn't want to think about it.*

His panic was only eased slightly when he saw somebody he recognised exit through the glass doors at the front of the building. His next-door neighbour.

"Hey! Excuse me!" he called, waving his hands to alert her.

The neighbour in question was a haggard woman in her 30s who had aged prematurely so much due to the environment and from stress that she looked about ready for death. She smelled like the stray cats she fostered and had a distracting staphylococcus infection covering her face. Bear had never learned her name but he'd seen her once leaving her home at the same time as he did.

She turned about at the sound of his voice, looking rather inconvenienced at him having called her.

"What?" She frowned back at him, in the usual discontent and chilly manner that was so common worldwide.

"Do you, by any chance, know what happened to the kid in number 3-D?"

"...Who are you?"

"Bea- I mean, Barret. Barret Orson."

"Oh, yeah, I remember you."

"So do you know what happened to my family?"

"Oh sure; I heard some noises yesterday morning through the wall. Sounded like the police. Some very official people anyway. Something about child neglect... extortion... foster care... I don't know, Smudge started whining for food then so I stopped listening. Now if you'll excuse me I'm a bit busy here," the neighbour announced before stepping into a parked run-down hatchback with one wing-mirror hanging off and starting the spluttering engine.

"Extortion?" Bear repeated in a horrified tone, his gazed fixed on the wall of the building with a frozen stare, "Foster care?"

Although he had been talking mostly to himself, Spider seemed to overhear him from the balcony.

"Sounds like your folks are in some big *trrrr*ouble!" Spider observed as he sucked his cheeks in, looking as if he was quite enjoying the excitement. He leaned his front over the balcony rails and looked down to Bear, "And I don't even know what extortion is!"

"I'm more concerned about the 'foster care' aspect of it," Bear told him, "That's got to be something to do with Ambrose."

"Well, there's a child placement thingy on the outskirts, maybe they know something about it."

"How do you know about that?"

"I know a lot of places around Eden."

"Well… I suppose it might be worth giving them a visit..." he admitted, though in reality he was inexplicably nervous about setting foot in the nicer parts of the city. Ambrose was a priority, though, and if he could get to the orphanage before a foster family adopted him… There might just be a chance… "Come on, Spider, let's go," he huffed.

"Where are we going?" Spider asked, swinging down neatly from the balcony to solid ground. He trotted quickly to keep up with Bear's wide strides as they made their way out of the back alleys.

"Home," Bear replied with a sigh, rubbing his temples, "I need to think some stuff over..."

The apartment bore a nipping chill as the evening sky darkened. Spider, leaving Bear to his thinking, had slipped away contently into the kitchenette area, where Spitfire stood with his back turned, pouring two iced teas. The floor lamp beside the counter provided a dim illumination to the room, but it still wasn't much.

"Oh, Spider, I was just about to come find you," Spitfire said, "Listen, I know we've had some misunderstandings, my guy, but I think it's time we made up."

He'd finished making the drinks by this point and had turned about with both cups in hand to face Spider. On his face he wore a friendly smile, an apologetic air about him.

Spider made eye contact, seeming sceptical but interested.

"Marcus told me you were helping Bear out with his little brother, and I think that's really..." (here Spitfire paused to try and remember the word he was looking for), "...Respectable. Y'know? So I thought 'hey, maybe this guy isn't so bad after all'. Reckon we could be buds?"

Spider tilted his head to the side and considered the proposition for a second. His eyes scanned over Spitfire's face and to the cup in his outstretched hand, as if trying to put his finger on the familiar air about him. Finally, he nodded his agreement and took the cup, watching as Spitfire breathed a sigh of relief.

"Hey, thanks, man," he said, "Maybe the atmosphere in here won't be so tense once we're best buds, huh?" and he laughed, awkwardly. He told Spider to enjoy his iced tea, gazed about the flat with a strange look on his face, and promptly left.

Chapter 9: Bleach and Trust

After thinking over the matter of going to the outskirts to finally locate his little brother, Bear had decided to go to bed early that evening and sleep on it. Spitfire had gone to stay at his friend's house, without revealing the name or address. Nobody questioned it. Only Marcus stayed awake, sitting on the other side of the room, on the couch, doing something very important with a file of papers.

As for Spider, he was silent as a mouse, curled up in the hammock. It wasn't clearly obvious whether he was awake or asleep.

Bear stirred in his half-asleep state as a pained groan came from Spider's direction.

"What's up?" he asked in a concerned tone, keeping his tired eyes closed.

"My throat..." Spider whined, *"Burns..."*

Bear sat up and looked across to the hammock.

"Did you scald yourself on something?"

"A different burn... My heart feels slow..."

At once remembering an incident from a few years ago, Bear sprung up out of bed and hurried to the kitchen. After supervising his little brother for a lot of his life, he had an inexplicable brotherly instinct to care for his new friend.

He re-entered the room swiftly with a great big glass of milk and commanded Spider to sit up.

"When Ambrose was really little, and I mean *really* little, he accidentally got into the cleaning cupboard and took a good gulp of bleach," he said, "I called poison control and they told me to give him milk. Lots of liquids. I did a lot of reading up about poisoning after that. I remember the symptoms."

"You think... I was poisoned?" Spider swallowed, looking dizzy.

"Well have you been sipping bleach?"

"Not that I can remember."

"Then it's the only alternative, isn't it?"

Spider stared blankly ahead, wondering when he could possibly have been poisoned. Then it dawned upon him.

"Spitfire."

"What about him?" Bear asked, carefully.

"He was acting weird..." Spider replied, shakily, "Gave me an iced tea. Tasted proper salty, I didn't finish it. Thought maybe it was off..."

An outrage kindling inside him, Bear gave a burning scowl. Something about Spitfire had rubbed him the wrong way ever since Spider mentioned their wordless enmity, but he never thought that he'd actually *do* anything.

Even having known Spider for less than a week, Bear felt an obligation to confront Spitfire immediately.

"As soon as he gets home," he glowered, placing a firm hand on Spider's tense shoulder, "I'm going to get to the bottom of this. Trust me."

"Thanks, Bear. You know, this all feels awfully familiar..."

Bear shot a glare to the doorway behind him, as if expecting the guilt-ridden flatmate to be standing there in silence and waiting. Of course, he wasn't, but Bear still looked. As soon at Spitfire walked through that door later he'd be there picking the bone.

Spider sighed, holding a hand over his aching abdomen, "I owe ya one..." he muttered, staring down blankly into the empty milk glass with a contemplative expression, "...I owe ya..."

Spitfire returned home mid-morning the next day when Spider was still resting, recovering from last night's ordeal. Marcus had been informed of the happenings earlier and had seemed reluctant to consider the possibility of his flatmate of four years poisoning someone, but the more he looked at the evidence, the more he had to admit it seemed plausible.

Rifling through the fridge, standing there like butter wouldn't melt in his mouth, Spitfire hummed a relaxed tune - *too* relaxed. He took a packet of roast chicken bites, shut the fridge door and turned about to immediately be confronted with a wide, towering figure.

"B- Bear! Hey!" he grinned, awkwardly, backing up against the fridge and almost losing his hold on the chicken, "How are you?"

"We need to talk."

"T- talk? About- about what? Is something wrong?"

"You bet your bottom dollar there is. What did you *do?"*

"Me?"

"What did you give him?"

"An… iced tea?"

"So you know what I'm talking about."

"Yes... I mean, no… Yeah?"

"Someone poisoned Spider, and it wasn't me or Marcus."

"What makes you think it was me?"

"He was here all day yesterday and it happened last night. You were the only one he accepted a drink from. Why did you think we wouldn't find out?"

Spitfire swallowed, anxiously, and stared up into Bear's eyes. He toyed with the packet in his hand. He didn't speak, but he had the same look on his face as a child who had just been caught with a shattered antique vase at his feet.

"Why did you do it?" Bear pushed.

"Me and Spider, we have a history," Spitfire retorted with a scowl.

"What kind of a history?"

"I can't tell you about it, OK? I told you, man, he's bad news. He always has been. He's a thief and a cheat."

Bear only stared down at him, disapprovingly, with an anger he couldn't quite explain. Spitfire hadn't wronged him personally but his actions felt like a cold stab in the heart regardless.

Marcus appeared not a few moments later with the same icy expression.

"Leyland," he said, using Spitfire's real name for once; a sure sign he was being deadly serious, "…*Attempted murder* is a

49

very serious crime. Don't think I won't call the police on you about this."

"I don't know who's the bigger idiot; you for doing something like this or me for not seeing it coming," Bear scowled at Spitfire as he turned away, rubbing the bridge of his nose.

Just as things seemed to be going so well – he was away from his parents, he had customers again and he got on alright with his new housemates – everything just fell apart. Ambrose was goodness-knows-where and now it had been revealed that a seemingly trustworthy acquaintance was a potential murderer. A bit of an unsubtle and careless one, but a killer nonetheless.

"You can't trust *anyone*, Barret," Spitfire told him, sourly, "I thought you'd know that. And pretty soon 'Spider' is gonna to back-stab you, too."

"I gotta' say, Bear, I really owe you one for what you did yesterday. I mean, confronting Spitfire like that? I couldn't have done it."

"You're welcome."

"I mean, if there's anything you need doing, I'll be more than happy to give you a hand. Maybe some chores, some shopping, fetching something that's fallen down the back of the cupboard. You name it!"

"I don't think that'll be necessary. But thanks."

"Well, I'm feeling a whole lot better now. A new get-up-and-go, y'know? I think we should go out and find Ambrose as soon as possible!"

Spider dropped down from the hammock like a stealthy cat and weaved over to where Bear was busy folding his clothes and packing them neatly into his bag.

"What are you doing?" he asked, pleasantly, still in a cheery mood.

"Packing," Bear replied, straight-faced. His face didn't usually show much outward emotion, but today even less so.

"Why?"

He paused, shirt in hand, and cast his gaze down to Spider, who was staring up at him with a sort of childlike innocence.

"Because I'm… I'm leaving, Spider."

Spider's expression shifted from curious to utterly shocked, with an offended air as if he'd just discovered that the dark web really exists.

"Leaving? Why?"

"Listen, what Spitfi- what Leyland said… was right. You can't trust anyone these days. I can't just find Ambrose and bring him back here, I wouldn't feel comfortable with it."

"So where are you going to go?"

"Sheltered accommodation, probably. I've looked into it."

Nodding slowly in understanding, Spider took a deep breath.

"Okay," he eventually agreed, "I'm cool with that, let's do it."

Bear heaved a sigh and softly placed a hand on Spider's shoulder,

"Spider… no. You can't come with me. I'm sorry."

"Why not? I thought we were friends."

"It's nothing personal, I just can't trust anybody to help me with this. I'm sorry, but it's just something that I have to face on my own."

It was, in fact, something personal. Although he didn't trust easily anyway, Spider was the most suspicious character he'd ever come across. Spitfire had called him a 'thief', and whether that was literal or metaphorical didn't matter, there was clearly a motive for murder in their so-called 'history'. Bear told himself quite strictly that didn't really care who Spider was any more, because what was really important was saving Ambrose from ending up in a home for the rest of his life (or, even worse, ending up with a family who didn't love him as much as they should). Ambrose needed to be with his big brother, that was all. He particularly didn't need to be surrounded by fishy characters like a supposed thief. The fact that Bear was inexplicably intrigued by Spider was just something he was going to have to put behind him.

He packed the last of his possessions snugly into his duffel-bag and zipped it shut with decisive speed. Before he turned to leave, he looked back to Spider one last time, and for a second the sadness in his fern-coloured eyes made him look oddly like Ambrose.

"If anyone comes to the door asking to get their devices fixed, tell them 'shop's closed', alright?" Bear said, straining a smile, "Take care."

He told himself that the sorrow in Spider's eyes was fake and made his way out of the room before he changed his mind, swinging the bag strap over his shoulder as he went.

Spider watched in a stunned silence as the only person who had ever been a friend to him walked away.

Silently, he opened the balcony doors and climbed up onto the roof with the intent of watching Bear's movements very closely indeed.

❈

Once again, Bear found himself on the murky streets of the city below, wandering aimlessly.

He'd never really spent much time in the city itself before, preferring to stay in the safety of his own home, where it was less likely that he would be attacked. The streets unnerved him. Everywhere he looked, something shady was going on. It wasn't just a matter of avoiding the worst places and thinking 'that's not the sort of thing that happens to me', as just about everybody in Eden had a story to tell about its vileness.

Marcus, when Bear had asked how he lost his finger, had told a rather scarring tale of fighting off a burglar back in his childhood home in downtown Kingston, Jamaica. His family had moved to Eden, he said, for the promises it made at the time. But when Bear asked him, he said that sometimes he wished he would have stayed put in Kingston.

Spider would have lots of stories to tell about Eden, Bear expected, if he'd ever speak about himself at all.

Bear had put on his best outfit, knowing he was going to the outskirts, and cleaned himself up as much as he could. Though he doubted he could keep totally neat and tidy after traversing the dirty streets.

Although his navigational skills were dodgy at best, Bear was determined to get out of central Eden and to the child placement offices where they would know the whereabouts of foster kids who had just been given a temporary home. Unfortunately, kids being given up by their parents (loving or unloving) for the sake of cost in Eden was a common issue. So much so that the offices had to be set up to manage all the fostering that went on. How Bear wished he could take them all under his wing… but that wasn't possible. He'd only be able to take Ambrose with him if he could prove that he was really his brother. That's why he'd brought ID: his Eden identity card, the only form he had (the city liked to keep tabs on exactly who resided in its borders and every child born would be issued with a card proclaiming their citizenship). He'd never owned a passport, nor had chance to obtain a driving license.

His plan was hurriedly thought through and decided upon, but despite the lingering feeling that he was forgetting something, Bear carried on walking away from home.

He was leaving behind something very desirable for the sake of finding Ambrose. An apartment right at the top of the building… it wasn't quite a luxury penthouse but a lot of people would kill for something like that. From the shockingly well-paid job of being a personal trainer (a lot of people wanted self-defence lessons nowadays and trainers were in high demand), Marcus had just been able to afford it, with help from his flatmates paying the rent. That's why furnishings were minimal, but it was worth it to keep away from the ground.

The ground was by far the worst part of the city. Especially the cordoned-off area where the air pollution was too high to not invest in a gas mask.

Bear felt a deep-rooted sorrow for those unfortunate enough to have to exist in that place. Existing… it wasn't living, not there. Nothing really felt like living any more. But maybe if things worked out, if he could get to Ambrose and move to the sheltered housing, maybe – just maybe – Ambrose would have a better chance at living than Bear had.

The average life expectancy in this part of Eden… fifty years old at best. As far as Bear was concerned, he was middle-aged by now. Again, he found his mind wandering to what existence would be like if he'd been born into better circumstances. But he ripped his mind away from it. Because there was no use sulking over things he couldn't ever have.

Breathing in the smoky air with a rasp, Bear bid goodbye to central Eden. He wouldn't miss it for a second.

The sound of a siren rang out through the streets (a common occurrence) and people shouted in anger, seemingly at the universe itself. Bear's foot met a puddle of oil as he left the grime for something better. Some*one* better. What else did he have left to live for if not his little brother?

He thought all about his early childhood as he wandered in the vague direction of the child placement offices. He'd never been to school, much like Ambrose, instead learning every skill he had from the Internet and from the very few lessons in reading and typing his parents had given him. Bright, although not particularly academically talented, young Barret turned his attentions to matters more practical: he learned to take apart and put back together small devices when he reached his early teens and developed a great interest in fixing little faults. As he watched the news and stared out of his bedroom window, it dawned on him just how vital it was to stand up for yourself in the modern world, and so started working out in the time he wasn't dissecting smartwatches. He'd have made a fine mechanic, he thought, if his parents could have afforded a car to let him work on.

Seeing his enthusiasm for fitness, the older teen in the flat beside his had given him his first set of weights when he and his family had to move, and they were the weights that Bear still had today. That older boy was the only thing close to a friend Bear had ever had.

Then, of course, came Ambrose.

Barret had very much been a parent to his younger brother, raising him as if he were his own son. With their parents too busy arguing about funds in the kitchen to pay attention to their crying baby, Barret stepped in. Cradling, feeding, singing as best he could. Anything he could find online about caring for a baby he put into practice.

As Ambrose grew, Barret was determined to give him the education he'd never received himself. Of course, school was out of the question, but learning by human interaction was not. And for those nine years, Ambrose and Barret were all each other had.

The nickname 'Bear' came both from Barret's appearance (tall, wide, much like a grizzly bear) and from the fact that, as he was learning to speak, 'Bear' was the closest Ambrose could come to Barret's name. It was all he called his older brother in later years, so it wasn't a surprise that it was the name Barret had chosen to take on when he started his 'new life' on his own.

Bear wondered how Ambrose was doing right this second, and his pace sped up involuntarily. If there were other kids at the foster home, were they nice to him? Were the parents caring? Somehow, Bear stayed hopeful. The faster he got to his brother, the better.

But then he thought about his parents in prison or wherever they were, and a spark of rage kindled a fire instantly in his stomach. How dare they treat their very own son the way they did… How *dare?* Had they no *empathy?* No hint of even a glimmer of parental love somewhere in their cold, hollow hearts? If Bear ever saw them again, he'd…

Well, he wasn't exactly sure *what* he'd do, but he knew it wouldn't be pleasant and might even be frowned upon by the authorities.

He hoped for his parents' sakes he never crossed paths with them again.

Sensing a sudden urgency to his mission, Bear felt his legs break into a run, seeing the buildings fly past him in a blur as he moved, weaving in and out between slow-walking souls shackled to the ground by their lack of a purpose. The weight of his duffel bag didn't hold him back. Bear believed he, for one, had an immediate purpose, and that if he didn't run he might never get the chance to fulfil it.

Far above the blinding lights of the city, above the stench and the smoke, above even the gigantic billboards, crouched a watchful figure dressed in deep red, looking out over the web of streets below.

Spider had perched himself on the edge of a relatively tall office block, where he could observe the happenings taking place on the streets, much like one of Eden's many surveillance cameras. They were everywhere nowadays, although crime was still rampant so they clearly weren't doing a very good job.

His eyes flashed like little green lasers over the city, waiting, and carefully he got down onto his front for stability, hanging his head over the side of the flat-topped building. Opposite the office block stood a tall, thin building with a neon sign that flickered out its name in glitchy red lettering. *The Arcady Hotel.* It had a reputation for being one of the worst budget hotels in the entire city, and those who stayed longer than one night usually emerged with a new disease to add to their collection. It was also the first you would encounter if you were entering central Eden from the outskirts near the vactrain station.

If Bear was on his way to the offices, Spider knew, he would definitely pass it. That was how he'd know if Bear was okay.

Minutes after Bear had left him alone in the flat, Spider had scuttled up to the roof and traversed the skyline to the very spot he reposed in now. For an hour now he had perched here, waiting for the tall figure of Bear to appear. Whether staying in the Arcady or just passing through, Spider didn't care, he just wanted to *see* him.

From the conversations they had had after first meeting, it was clear Bear hadn't spent a lot of time on the streets themselves. The city's maze of winds and turns would unquestionably be confusing for somebody who had never before journeyed through the concrete jungle.

Spider stretched out to relax, lounging on the roof. He knew he'd be here a while, and he was already getting restless. Just an hour more, he thought… then he'd know something was wrong. So, after pulling out a chocolate bar he had stuffed in one of the pouches of his utility belt, Spider kept his eyes firmly trained on the street of the Arcady Hotel.

Whether he cared to admit it or not, it was a fact that Bear was well and truly lost. The years he spent indoors had resulted in a complete lack of directional sense, which he now had to face the consequences of.

Every street in the city looked exactly the same. Every run-down shop and dirty back street and broken car looked identical to the one before it. The online map that Bear had regarded led him only to the barbed wire fencing of the cordoned-off area. Unless he wanted to catch three terminal illnesses, he couldn't go any further.

Sighing loudly, he once again looked down to consult his map, but as his eyes met the screen he was confronted with the announcement that his phone battery had fallen to one percent before the screen abruptly went black. He stared down at it for a minute in silence, defeated. Of all the things he could have forgotten, charging his device was not one he had expected. With a battery life of a grand two days, he wasn't used to having to set it down to sleep very often. Of course, having it on full brightness as he wandered helplessly around the inner city did not help

Sliding it into his pocket in silence, he made a mental note to stop by at the next public charging station he saw and carried on in a direction that just felt *right,* hoping to find something like a signpost or maybe a friendly elf who would point him in the right direction.

Turning right down a street of mostly unlit shops, Bear found himself staring down the alley to a lanky figure a few meters away. Though not quite friendly elf material, Bear stepped forward towards him.

"Excuse me?"

The figure, wearing a tattered jacket with a hazard symbol on the back (showing that he came from the confines of the fenced-off, high pollution area – a slightly insulting sign to bear, but a mandatory one) turned to face him. His mouth and nose were covered in a large, double canister gas mask to stop the spread of diseases he might be carrying and his glassy eyes gazed back at Bear with a look of surprised exhaustion.

"Do you… Do you by any chance know the quickest way to the outskirts?" Bear asked, his heart pumping at an alarming frequency.

Through the breathy rasp of the canisters, a gravelly voice croaked out a reply.

"The outskirts?.. I haven't been there in a long time…" he seemed to contemplate his own sentence for a while before finally carrying on, pausing every few words to draw another loud breath, *"I don't know the whole way there… but if you carry on down that last street… take a left down Felicity Street… carry on until you get to this real wide alleyway… that's a shortcut to the Arcady Hotel. They can give you directions there… If the staff are in a good mood."*

Bear nodded slowly in understanding,

"OK, got it. Thank you."

"Just be careful of the dogs."

"Dogs?"

"Yeah there used to be a dogfighting ring around there… some of the hounds still stick around… 'cause of the butcher's shop."

"Dogfighting?"

"Don't sound so surprised… it got shut down a month or so back… don't you read the news?"

"I try not to."

"That's probably wise… where you heading to, anyway?"

"Just… trying to find someone."

Although he looked curious, even a touch suspicious, the shady character didn't push any more questions. He seemed to know when to stop asking.

"Well… Just be careful… okay? Those shiny window displays might look good… but it's no place for people like us."

Swallowing, Bear gave another nod. He knew exactly what this implied. He thanked the figure one last time and turned to leave.

"*One last thing.*"

"Hm?" he hummed, gazing back over his shoulder.

There was a short pause before any continuation.

"*I wouldn't buy anything from the butcher's if I were you.*"

"...I think I know what you mean."

Just as Bear was beginning to believe that the hazardous area and the sorry excuses for streets that surrounded it were the worst part of the city, he was confronted with the horror that was a back alley. It was the last step in getting to the Arcady Hotel, and even though the end was in sight, this alley was making the idea of turning around and going back home sound like an extremely appealing option.

Bear tripped over his own feet as a bout of explosive barking from behind startled him, and his hand flew to clutch his heart. This shortcut was making him wish he'd taken a 'long-cut' instead. His only company as far as he knew was a rusty bicycle and a large bin.

Composing himself and getting over his initial shock, Bear looked around for the source of the incessant barking and soon set eyes upon a Rottweiler of unsettlingly thin stature with crusty eyes and hackles raised. It didn't look particularly well cared for, but then, it was hard to keep yourself in good health in a place like this, never mind your animals. And this one was probably feral like the ones the helpful stranger had mentioned.

"*Hey there...*" Bear started, nervously stepping backwards, "Good doggy... *Goood* doggy..."

Alas, it was not a 'good doggy', unsurprisingly. It held its head level to its shoulders and emitted a deep growl that seemed to judder Bear's heart like a baby's rattle. With an abrupt bark, it jumped forward, clearly intent on sinking its teeth into the first thing available.

Bear stumbled rearward and his back met the wall behind with a harsh thud. He slid down it as his knees buckled and he ended his descent on the ground in a very cold puddle. He'd never really encountered a dog this close before, and he'd certainly never had one attack him.

"Easy, boy," he shakily begged, "Down! Lie down! Sit!"

His commands had no effect, and the Rottweiler only lurched forward to grab him by the leg, seizing the material of Bear's tracksuit trousers with yellow teeth. From such a close angle, Bear could see the thick snot dripping from the hound's nostrils and the eye crust that looked like bits of honey-nut cornflakes.

Knowing no better, Bear let a shout of terror escape him as he tried to pull himself away, the result of which was smacking the back of his skull against the brickwork behind him.

He yelled for help at the top of his lungs – although the area was barren – trying to kick the dog off with his spare leg at the same time as reaching up to touch the back of his head with his hand. As he drew his palm away and looked down at it with blurred vision, he saw the smearing of blood on his fingertips.

Being torn to shreds by an angry Rottweiler in a back alley behind a butcher's shop was not the way Bear thought that he would depart this mortal coil, but here he was.

The dog in question had a vice-like hold on his right leg and looked to have no intention of letting go any time soon. Furiously, it shook his leg about like a limp rag doll until its teeth sank through the trouser fabric and met skin.

Letting it happen, more or less, Bear tried not to wriggle, too distracted by the pain in the back of his head. If he survived this, he reckoned he'd end up with a nasty concussion. Vision swirling around him as if he was looking through a fish tank, Bear shielded his face with his arm and willed the ordeal to be over. But just as he was ready for his limbs to be torn off his body, he felt a weight lift from him.

A weak yelp was heard and a few more barks before the light scurrying of paws on concrete. Something heavy and metal fell to the floor with a clash.

Bear groaned in pain as his vision started to recalibrate itself and his hand reached out to hold his stinging shin.

"Get up. Quick."

He raised his eyes, woozily, to see who had spoken, and there stood a small figure with a utility belt on his hips and a rusty bicycle at his feet.

"Spider?" Bear managed to say, weakly.

"Come on, can you stand?"

"I… I don't know."

"Try it. Scared that pooch off for now but I'm sure he'll be back for round two soon enough. We gotta get moving before that happens."

"What are you doing here?" Bear asked him, disregarding the entire preceding sentence, as he used the bin beside him to pull himself to his feet. As his weight came to rest on his injured leg, a shooting agony flew up the entire right side of his body.

"Just looking out for an old pal," Spider replied, looking him up and down with an air that was either disappointment or concern.

"You were stalking me?"

"To make sure you were OK."

"And you didn't think to drop by and give me some help?"

"You didn't look like you wanted anything to do with me when you gallivanted off earlier."

Bear admitted he couldn't argue with this.

"Sorry."

"No, it's cool. Where are you heading?"

"To the 'Arcady Hotel', I've been advised. For directions."

"You shouldn't walk any further today. Not on that leg. We'll head down to the hotel but we're staying the night," Spider told him, very matter-of-factly, turning to lead the way to said hotel.

"We?" Bear repeated, questioningly.

Spider stared back over his shoulder at his huge form, standing there in that alley like a defeated soldier, a rip in his trousers and the same look on his face that a child might make after just being told their goldfish died.

"You're not so tough… are you, big guy?"

Bear swallowed.

"...Guess not, huh?"

"I'm coming with you the rest of the way," Spider announced, "Just to the offices. Then… Then if you don't want to see me, that's fine. As long as you're safe. You and your little brother."

"Why?"

"...Just because. Come on, or do you want your other leg mauled too?"

"I'm coming," Bear nodded, and started to limp after him.

The Arcady Hotel, tall, thin, woebegone and crumbling, in any other situation would have been something to give a wide berth to. But if it meant getting off the back streets and away from the dogs, Bear could just about put up with it.

Spider led him to the front doors in a lively gait, unsurprising for his personality but still slightly jarring. Bear had never met

someone so unsettlingly positive. The merry mystery pushed open
the door, which creaked in protest and slammed closed thereafter.

Upon entering the bleak lobby, Bear was greeted with an
unforgettably grim stench; a wondrous aroma of mould, alcohol,
ammonia and mystery meat with a little something else sprinkled in
for good measure. Bear held his breath before his insides became his
outsides.

The lobby itself – a sorry excuse of a room – was dimly lit
and sparsely furnished. A neon sign in the window proclaimed there
were (unfortunately) vacancies. The ceiling was yellowed and the
plaster on the walls was peeling and cracking like dermatitis,
collecting in little scaly piles on the floor tiles. Against one flaky
wall sat a sad faux leather couch with one leg missing (now propped
up with a small plastic crate) which nobody in their right mind would
sit on. The vending machine was empty save from a single bottle of
suspicious-looking grape-flavoured energy drink, and the reception
desk was unmanned.

"Boy, this place looks like it came straight from the
twenties..." Bear muttered, covering his mouth and nose with his
arm, "Couldn't hurt them to refurbish a bit."

Spider rang the buzzer on the desk and his finger came away
upsettingly sticky.

A minute passed before anybody came to help him. A man
appeared, tall and thin, bags under his eyes and an irritable scowl
upon his pockmarked face. He spoke no words, but got out a tattered
guest book from a shelf in the desk and looked expectantly down at
Spider.

"Double room," Spider said, and then added on a delayed
'please'. If you displayed manners around these parts, you'd be
looked on like you were an outsider. Vulnerable, naive even.

The man – seemingly the only staff member in the building –
jotted this down in his little book and aggressively informed Spider
of the price.

Spider looked straight back over his shoulder to Bear.

"You brought money, right?"

"Uh... yeah… yeah, of course," Bear replied, coming to his senses and fumbling around in his bag for his old wallet.

After shakily and reluctantly parting with his money, Bear was pointed towards a messily carpeted staircase that led to the ominously dark hallway above.

Spider wasted no time in starting on his way to room A-5, however Bear paused at the bottom of the stairs, disinclined to climb with his bad leg. Feeling the staff member's eyes drilling into him he painfully lifted his leg and began to drag himself upwards, wincing at every step. He reached for the handrail.

"I wouldn't grab that rail if I were you," Spider warned, and Bear retracted his hand immediately.

The stench somehow got more pungent as he made his way up to the corridor, spreading its taste on the back of his throat, bitter and acrid. Trying to ignore it, Bear blew a sigh and choked on dust as he breathed back in. He dreaded to think what this atmosphere was doing to his lungs.

Spider presented the wooden door with his keycard and it made an uncomfortable bleep as it unlocked, and creaked as it opened like a warning to those unfortunate enough to enter.

"Well, here we are!" Spider proclaimed, straining a smile.

Bear limped over to look over his shoulder and held back a gag as his eyes were forced to observe the filth inside.

"We're supposed to… stay here?"

"Oh come on, it's not *that* bad," Spider tried to reassure him, "I don't even see anything moving yet."

"M-moving?"

"Yeah, you know, like carpet beetles, bed bugs, dust mites, cockroaches..."

Bear swallowed, nervously, as he followed Spider into the room, shutting the door behind him. He suddenly felt rather trapped.

"What even *is* that *smell?*"

"What smell, Bear?"

"Can't you smell it? It's like… I can't even describe it..."

"Is this, by any chance, your first time in a hotel?"

Bear was silent, almost guiltily.

"I thought so," Spider nodded, "Just don't let that wound of yours touch anything," he cautioned, giving a small laugh, "You never know *what* you're going to find in a place like this."

Bear leaned against the wall, feeling the wallpaper damp against his back, his leg stinging as if he'd taken a dip in a pit of acid. He reached down a hand to part the ripped fabric and hold his shin.

"Let's see… What have we here?" came Spider's voice from the other side of the room, but Bear didn't look up to see him. He was far too distracted by studying his wound.

He could see where the dog's teeth had sunk in and it made his stomach turn… The next thing he knew, a tube of antiseptic cream was being presented to him along with a bandage.

"Put this on. It'll help stop that nasty thing getting all yucky and infected."

Bear tentatively took the first aid supplies and looked at them with a melancholy air. His little quest so far had not gone to plan, and the city had not treated him quite as kindly as he'd hoped when he set off.

He finally raised his line of sight as Spider started to walk away, still rummaging through the various compartments on his bulky utility belt.

"Spider," Bear started, weakly, just loud enough for him to hear.

"Hm?"

"…Thanks."

Spider's faced cracked into a cheerful grin, his pointed teeth showing.

"You're welcome!" he smiled.

Bear began to fix up his wound, wincing every time a thread of fabric brushed past the bite marks. He'd always believed that if he looked tough he could fend for himself, but now he was finding out that the city didn't discriminate. It didn't matter how tall he was or how many push-ups he'd done, hungry dogs don't care if you look tough. And neither did disease.

After ensuring his leg was safely wrapped, Bear took a moment to observe his surroundings a bit. He rose to his feet, shakily, and limped to the barred window to gaze out over the city he regrettably resided in. Being as lost in thought as he was, he didn't even hear Spider get down on his hands and knees and proclaim that 'hey, there's a needle down here!'.

"Spider, do you ever wonder… whether this is all there is?"

"...To the hotel?" Spider replied, without looking up to him, "No, there's loads more rooms. You haven't even looked around this one proper yet."

"No, not to the hotel," Bear sighed, "To... you know..."

"...Do I?"

"To life, Spider."

"Oh. I don't know about that, Bear."

There was a squeak of floorboards and a jingle of belt buckles as Spider rose to his feet and made his way over, every step prompting a creak of protest from the floor.

Bear leaned his strong arms on the tall windowsill and Spider stood on his tiptoes to do the same.

"There's more in the world than just this city. If you watch the news-"

"I don't watch the news any more," Bear put in before he could finish, "I don't believe what they say."

Spider paused for a moment, chewing the inside of his mouth.

"It's not good. Here, I mean. In Eden. And it's not very good in other places either. But there are still nice things out there. Y'know, where people haven't… built up much."

Bear didn't reply. His eyes were fixed on the streets outside.

Their room faced away from the back alley they had escaped from minutes before. Instead, they were treated to a view of a gap between buildings that stretched right to the outskirts where the lights were brighter and the buildings were taller. Strangely enough, going there seemed like more of an intimidating thought than going back to that alley.

"I've heard of a little place," Spider continued, "It's not far from here. A little village. Where there's lots of good people and there's trees and everything."

Bear gave a sharp snort of amusement before finally turning his head to look down at Spider.

"You really believe that?"

Spider's face fell and he swallowed.

"You don't?"

"I think it's just something that we get told to… what's the word… 'keep the dream alive'? To make it seem like this isn't all there is to life, that there's still some good people out there and that somewhere the skies are blue instead of grey. But I don't believe it. I mean, with all the pollution and- and the state of the monetary system? And what, there's an old traditional pub or something with classical music?" Bear told him, "I might have believed it when I was a kid, but that's just the thing; it seems childish... What do you think?"

Spider was silent for a good few seconds of contemplation. The cogs in his brain were methodically turning, gradually loading a cohesive sentence.

"I think there's no point saying something is a lie without proof," he said eventually, "I think… there's no point in carrying on if you don't look for something to hope for."

With a gentle raise of the brow, Bear pulled a rather impressed expression.

"That's very profound of you, Spider."

"Thank you."

"I've never known you to say so many words all at once."

"Neither have I," Spider replied with a slight smile and stepped away.

Bear's eyes found their way back to the window, where the cracked glass was sending a biting chill over his face. Absent-minded, his gaze trained itself on a fat bluebottle fly making its way up one of the iron bars on the other side of the glass. Must be easy being a fly in a place like this.

"...Spider, there's something I've been meaning to ask."

The padding of Spider's footsteps on the threadbare rug ceased as he heard this.

"I was trying to edge around it. Didn't want to say it directly..." (here Bear turned to face him), "...But who *are* you?"

A pair of glassy green eyes stared back at him, thoughtful.

The silence was heavy and Bear started to wonder whether he should have asked the question at all. But just as he was about to say 'forget it', he got his answer.

"I don't know."

"...What?"

"I said I don't know."

"Can you elaborate?"

"Look, Bear, I don't want to bore you. I gave you the long and short of it. You don't want to hear me go on and on. You think I'm a freak, that's why you wouldn't let me come with you."

"I... didn't mean to come across like that, Spider, I'm sorry. But we're both here now and I want to listen."

Spider sat himself down on the end of one of the beds, still looking sceptical.

"...Bear, I woke up one day..."

Here he paused, thinking.

'As you do,' Bear thought, but stayed silent.

"I... I didn't know where I was. I was cold. Everything hurt, especially my head. Had nothing but the clothes on my back. I just laid there wondering how to stand up. When I picked myself off the floor, I dragged myself to somewhere I thought I could hide. I didn't know much, but I knew I had to find some way to look after myself."

"Go on."

"...I thought that I'd remember where I lived and who I was and who my friends were. But I didn't. I didn't know anyone. I don't know anything. Everything I have, I've had to scavenge for. Including food. One day... Marcus... he saw me looking for something to eat. Guess he felt sorry for me. Took me back to his place, gave me whatever he could spare. I went back whenever I had nowhere else to go. Spitfire didn't like that."

"He didn't like Marcus giving you food?"

Spider shook his head firmly.

"I suppose he felt really strongly about it to go to the extent of trying to poison you," Bear hummed.

"I don't think that was it."

"You don't?"

"He didn't like me at all, but he never would tell me why. I don't think it matters now. We don't have to deal with him any more."

Bear still wasn't content to accept this as an answer and move on. He knew that people did things without reasoning sometimes, but he just couldn't accept that Spitfire would attempt to kill Spider just because Marcus fed him occasionally. There was definitely something going on, but it seemed that Spider was just as lost as Bear was, so he didn't push questions.

"I'm sorry about what happened to you, Spider," he said, leaning back on the windowsill and sighing, "And I'm sorry I was so harsh on you at first."

"That's okay," Spider replied in his usual brief manner.

"Hey, maybe we can... work together from now on. No more of the 'every man for himself' thing."

Spider's blank expression shifted then into a grateful but weak smile. He made himself comfy and nodded his head,

"I think I'd like that."

"Friends?" Bear offered, stretching out an arm.

"Friends," Spider answered, shaking his hand in a very decisive manner.

<u>Chapter 13: Panda Eyes</u>

Bear's waking thoughts ran as follows:
'What's that smell?'
'Where am I?'
'My leg is burning...'
'No really what's that smell?'
'Is there something crawling on me or is it just a shiver?'
He cracked his eyes open and stared down to his arm to locate the source of the tickle and soon located something with many legs crawling up his forearm. Immediately, he sprang into an upright position, letting a yelp escape him as he flailed his arm around in a mild panic.

"I see you have met Robert the Roach," said a voice from the bathroom doorway.

Bear, now free from the creepy crawly's grasp, put his hand to his forehead and rubbed his temples firmly. His rough awakening from a terrible night's sleep had not started his day off with sunshine and rainbows. He gradually raised his eyes to look to Spider in the doorway.

"...Robert?" he uttered eventually, regarding Spider's prior comment.

"Yeah, Robert the Roach. His whole gang is here in the bathroom. I found their home. It's a right party."

"That's *horrible,* Spider!" Bear retorted, getting out of bed as quickly as humanly possible and scanning the sheets for any other unwelcome visitors, "Well, we have to tell the owners!"

"I wouldn't," Spider replied, casually neatening his sleeves, "They don't take well to criticism."

Bear swallowed, his saliva feeling like pinpricks down the back of his throat. *What had he breathed during the night...? Probably a whole family of dust mites...*

"We better get outta' here," Spider told him, "Don't wanna get in trouble for overstaying our welcome."

"Is the room really booked in for that short a duration?"

"Busy area."

As soon as Bear's foot met the floor and the slightest bit of weight was placed upon it, a shooting pain shredded the muscle from his shin to his ankle. Wincing, he suppressed the urge to cry out in pain and instead hung his head to grit his teeth in secret.

"You don't have to hide it," Spider told him, suddenly losing his upbeat spark.

"I'm fine," Bear insisted.

Spider was silent, and it was clear that he could see through the brave front.

"I'm not taking you to any hospital or what around these parts," he said, flatly, "They're terrible. When we get to the outskirts. Then we'll go to… A and E or something. Just keep it bandaged and you might not get rabies."

"Thanks, Spider," Bear sighed before rising to his feet with a pained wobble. He limped his way to the bathroom as Spider's sharp eyes followed his movements like icy lasers.

The reflection in the mirror stared back at Bear with a gaze of soulless disappointment. His eyes were ringed with purple to the extent he could have changed his alias to Panda, and his skin had turned a shade he'd only ever seen through milk bottles. Resting gently on the basin, Bear leaned in to inspect a burst blood vessel in his eye that had spattered his sclera with crimson. When the basin started to pull away from the wall, Bear quickly removed his weight. There was something about himself that he noticed as he stared, transfixed. He looked… *off;* his skin a shade too pale, his eyelids a bit too tired, his shoulders a touch too lax. As if he wasn't himself any more. He wasn't Barrett Orson and he wasn't the sure, confident Bear he thought he was, either. He didn't exactly know who this new person was. And he noticed, with a mix of dismay and fellow feeling, that with the pallidness and the panda eyes, he was beginning to look oddly like Spider.

Snapping back to his senses as best he could, Bear ran the cold water tap, ignoring the screeching sound it emitted as he did so, and dunked his hands to wash his face. The water itself had a certain aroma to it that didn't exactly scream 'clean', but it was the only thing available.

He left the room in the same daze as he'd entered it in, half-dragging his bad leg behind him as he pulled himself over to the bag which contained his clothes. When he got to see his brother again, he knew, he'd start looking like himself again.

In an odd sort of way, the feeling of Spider being there in the corner had a kind of reassuring air. And although Bear still wasn't sure who this individual was, there was something familiar about him, as if somewhere along the line they'd gone through the same thing.

Out on the streets, Bear felt strangely less vulnerable than he had in the hotel. The air at least wasn't stuffy and still like it was inside.

He hadn't been this far away from home in a long time, this close to the outskirts. In his resolve to never step foot outside the confines of his home unless absolutely necessary, he had tried to never stray farther than a few streets away. He thought that what he'd seen there had been bad enough, but in this short yet eventful time lately he had seen things that he hadn't thought could even exist so close to where he resided.

Dog fighting rings, for example, he believed were a thing of the past, up until that stranger warned him of the hounds that still roamed the alleys. Then it all became a touch too real.

That was what had changed him, he reckoned. The knowledge that what had once been something he subconsciously knew was going on was now affecting him very personally.

"Spider, I..."

They hadn't spoken for a good while, and Bear was (as usual) the first to break the silence.

"Hmm?"

"Before this all happened, before my parents kicked me out of the house… I don't think I realised what it was really like out here. I'd see reports about rises in unemployment… homelessness… and I'd think… 'that's really terrible'… but I don't know if it sunk in that it was real. Then… well, I realised that it's really happening. It's been a bit of a smack in the face, really, to be thrown in at the deep end of what I'd tried to turn a blind eye to for so long… *Ah-* look at me; I'm rambling again."

"Me too."

"…What was that?"

"I said 'me too'," Spider repeated, "Although I don't know what I was like before… you know. When I came to, I was- Well. 'Thrown in at the deep end' like you said."

"What happened to you was awful. But I'm glad to know that we share an experience."

Spider looked like he was about to add something more, but before he could speak, an unearthly thump echoed throughout the central city and everything was plunged into darkness.

At first, Bear thought he might have fainted. But he soon gathered that he was still on his feet, and his eyes slowly adjusted to the darkness. Through the gaps in the buildings, he could see a purple light filtering through, nothing but fine lines creeping through the darkness.

"Power cut," Spider said, and he sounded rather serious, "We'd better get some light."

Although it was morning, scaffolding and other overhead obstructions ensured no daylight from the clouded skies could creep through. Much like most days. It seemed almost like the bowels of the city had been *designed* to be unpleasant. The electrics themselves in these areas were wired on a completely different grid to the outskirts. To save on costs, or maybe to make them look even bleaker than they already were. *If you work hard,* Eden would tell its inhabitants, *you can move up in the world.* Get to the nicer parts of the city. Be part of the one percent. Have better lights maybe. The grime, Bear figured, was supposed to be motivation.

Spider fumbled around in his belt's pockets for a bit before bringing out a keyring LED and flicking it on.

Immediately, an impressively wide, bright beam of light spread across the ground in front of them, illuminating a crushed cola can and a damp cardboard box.

"I found this in the garbage. Pretty nifty, huh?" Spider smiled, proudly.

Bear strained a smile in return, his heart still thumping like a rock concert with an overzealous audience. The bangs in his chest made his entire body flinch, and when Spider looked up at him it seemed to be with an air of amusement.

"Don't worry. We have light; we should be safe. Power cuts are dangerous. Bad guys think it's a good time to strike. But you get used to it."

Bear had witnessed power cuts before, but he had been inside, safe and sound, at those times. Usually he had his curtains closed anyway. When it was dark in the flat, he'd be the one to comfort his terrified younger sibling. Pull him onto his knee and tell him there was nothing to worry about. And they'd read something in the darkness, a screen illuminating their faces and nothing else. Back then he'd had to be courageous for the sake of the child, so in a way Ambrose had made him braver. But he didn't have that any more.

He wondered how Ambrose was feeling in this moment. Was he scared still? Did he have someone there who was reading with him right now?

"Hello? Ey, ted-bear? Anyone home?"

Spider's voice snapped Bear back to the moment, and he found himself staring straight into the round eyes of his travelling companion. The LED was also training its beam right onto his face, giving him a rather unflattering under-chin glow.

"Sorry," he said, clearing his throat, "Just drifted off a bit."

"I told you, don't worry. Come on, no power is no reason to stop. Stay in the light."

Bear followed along close behind, and he wondered whether Spider looked at him the same way he himself looked at poor helpless Ambrose.

<u>Chapter 14: Neon</u>

Marcus Morris had never really been fazed by anything that happened to him.

Losing his finger while getting robbed? Well, he'd recovered from that pretty fast. What was one finger when he still had nine left?

Housemates coming and going, with their dodgy personalities and shady activities? Marcus had just come to accept that he was practically the manager of a hotel now rather than a room-mate.

His father's death back when Marcus was in his teen years? Well, he told himself, that's just life, isn't it?

But something about this recent situation was just… getting to him.

For once, he found himself alone in the apartment, the only occupant. That in itself didn't bother him so much, but the fact that everyone had disappeared so suddenly he couldn't help but find quite jarring.

That was when a knocking caught his attention and he quickly flicked soap suds off his hands, snatching up a tea towel as he moved over to answer the door. To his surprise (and disappointment), the person at the door was none other than his most aggravating tenant.

"What are you doing here?" Marcus frowned, still drying his hands.

"Hey, I just came to, y'know, apologise and all that-"

"Leyland. This ain't a matter of saying sorry and everything being fine."

"Aw, c'mon Marcus you're a good dude I know you are."

"Which is why I called the police; they're looking out for you. How have they not found you yet?"

Leyland tapped his nose,

"I don't get caught that easy," he smirked, "So let me in and we can talk this through. What happened isn't who I am. Where's Bear?"

"I don't know, he left. And I'm not letting you in, either," Marcus scowled.

Leyland's expression turned sour and he leaned in closer to whisper.

"They're right on my tail, can't I just… slip inside a minute? I'll be out of here before you know it I promise!"

"You're fortunate I didn't just call the cops on you and keep you here until they arrived when I found out what you'd done. I gave you a chance, even if I'm starting to regret it. you can't just come running back to me."

"Marcus-"

"No, I've sheltered some bad people in my time, but that ends now," Marcus snapped before shutting the door with an unmistakable air of firmness.

Even as he turned away he could hear the thumping of Leyland's fists upon the plastic and the repeated calls of his name. But he didn't turn back around again.

He didn't know why, but he had a notion deep down… even though he knew nothing about Spider and had known 'Spitfire' for longer, he had a feeling that he didn't want to be on Leyland's side.

"Let there be light!"

The city's illuminations powered on with the same thunderous clanging that they had departed with. Blinding light harshly extinguishing the darkness that had flooded the streets before it.

Bear put his arm quickly over his face to save his poor retinas from being burned alive, and when he had finally recovered, slowly looked downwards to Spider.

Spider himself looked rather unbothered by the whole thing and after his single comment went about putting his little LED back in his utility belt pouch.

"Attention all citizens! Eden City apologises for the short lack of power you just experienced," came a loud, sugar-sweet voice from every corner of the city all at once.

Bear stared upwards to see the lofty billboard screens on the tops of buildings illuminated with the face of a professional-looking lady wearing cat-eyed glasses and some rather striking makeup.

"We understand this may have caused some inconveniences..."

Spider stood there neatening his clothes, miming along to the announcement as if he'd heard it a hundred times before.

"We hope that this short music broadcast will restore some cheer. Remember: work hard, earn hard, be the one percent."

And with that, the screens returned to their usual poster advertisements as the sound of *'Downtown'* by Petula Clark started playing merrily through the speakers.

"C'mon, Bear, let's get going," Spider chirruped, nodding his head to the buildings where the pinkish light had leaked through minutes before.

"I hated that," Bear said, blankly, eyes still fixed on the advertisements.

"...The power cut?"

"The announcement. They just don't care, do they?"

"Well, no, Bear; we do live in the dumps. Now come on-"

"They act as if everything is fine. Did you see how she smiled? How cheery she sounded? 'Restore some cheer', she said, as if there was cheer in the first place! How privileged-"

"Bear-"

"I mean, to have the *audacity* to say they're sorry as if we'd actually believe them? It was their fault the whole time, they purposefully made everything here worse just to make themselves feel above us. To act as if-"

"Bear."

He stopped mid-way through his sentence and stared down at Spider's face gazing back up at him. He looked unperturbed, but stern, maybe even a little weary.

"There's no use in getting angry," he said, flatly, "We didn't set off to change the world. Or… overthrow the conglomerate, or whatever. We set off for Ambrose."

Bear heaved an exhausted sigh, running a hand over his pale face and letting the base of his palm rest over one eye.

"Yeah, you're… you're right…" he muttered. He hated to admit it, but there was nothing really he could personally do about the state of the world they lived in. And in the whole of the kid's life, Ambrose probably couldn't do anything either.

He couldn't help thinking back to the man he met the day before, dressed in that tattered coat, face covered in a gas mask. The toxic symbol on the back of the coat was not just a warning to others not to get too close, but another excuse for those better off to feel good about themselves. Because even in the shady hotels, the smelly alleyways and the run-down apartments, people of Bear's class still needed someone to look down on. At least, that's what the people in charge believed. If they could add another, even lower, class to sneer at, they probably would.

Bear followed Spider in a bit of a trance, still pondering over his thoughts, kicking the occasional beer bottle out of his path as he went. Was there even any point in getting Ambrose back? He wouldn't get out of the city. He wouldn't have a chance at a better life or an education – the thought of him going to college made Bear laugh internally – so what was the reason? Wasn't pulling him out of wherever he was now to go and live in grimy sheltered housing just *selfish* on Bear's part?

He would have stopped in his tracks and sat down on the floor to think about it longer, to tell himself how foolish and self-centred he had been, but the rhythm of his own footsteps had him hypnotised.

"Hey… Spider?"

"Yes?"

"That place that you were talking about… the village. With the nice people and the trees."

"What of it?"

"Do you really believe in it?"

"Do you really not believe in it?"

"That's not what I asked."

"There are destination posters in the vac-train station for the place. And you think they just… go to nowhere?"

"I've never been in the station, Spider. I don't go to places I don't belong."

"If you don't... keep a belief that there's something better out there in your mind, then there's nothing to hope for. And if you have nothing to hope for you have nothing to live for. So even if it seems like a little thing, you have to find hope in something."

"...You can be a real Plato sometimes, you know that?"

"A what?"

"Never mind. Just keep walking."

<u>Chapter 15: Canis Lupus</u>

It wasn't long until the magenta light grew brighter and the sounds of traffic grew louder. The ambience of the outskirts, bright and glossy, blinding even, came into view like light at the end of the tunnel.

Bear didn't think he'd ever come back here after his experience the last time. It was the last time, in fact, that he had strayed further than a few streets from home. He was sixteen, hardly as strong as he was currently, and a good few inches shorter. His parents weren't home at the time, as usual, working their long hours at the factory. They'd told him that he'd have to get a job in one of the three Eden Corp sweatshops soon, start earning his keep. His protest had been to run away from home, so he'd packed his bag with the majority of his belongings and convinced someone in a car outside to give him a lift to the outskirts.

It had seemed a fine idea then. He'd saved his money for a hostel and planned to get together with other travellers he'd meet there, live out of a suitcase maybe, hop about. But within the first hour of his time in the place, a group of three boys around his age in designer gear had kicked him to the side of the road, stolen his bag and called him some things he couldn't repeat.

Injured and disheartened, he'd spent his money on a ride back home before his big 'journey' had even begun and hadn't been back since.

Now, as he emerged into the bright lights of the world of the one percent, his brain flashed up images of that time on the backs of his eyes. He thought he could go out on his own back then and he'd thought it recently, too. Had he learned nothing, he wondered? He definitely never expected the one thing that saved him to be a five foot four stranger with a grappling hook and no name.

The smell of the inner city's garbage, chimneys and sick faded away a bit and were replaced with the bitter scent of bleach and warm food from cleaner eating-places along the street. The buildings were brighter, no scaffolding holding everything together or broken vents on the walls rattling as they pushed out foul air. What would have been rows of old doors lining the sides of the buildings were here flashy billboards or floor-to-ceiling windows for the residents of the apartments.

Any access points to the inner city were nothing but narrow alleyways barely large enough for a single vehicle, and people didn't give them a second glance. Invisible. Insignificant. And that's how Bear felt, too, when he stood there.

"*Prrr*etty stylish, hm?" Spider droned, admiring the towering glass buildings.

Almost every light around was illuminated with a bright purple hue, sometimes interrupted by a dash of light blue. It was a stark contrast to the dark yellow ambience of the inner city.

"Yeah," Bear replied flatly, distracted, "Really modern..."

"Come on. Can't stand and gawk all day."

Spider tapped Bear's arm with the back of his hand to alert him and started on his way down the street. Bear followed, though his eyes still wandered to the scenery.

There was a lot more traffic around, streets were wider and there was a good amount of pedestrians walking around. They dressed wildly different from people in the other parts, too. Their clothes were tight fitting, sometimes all-in-one pieces, with the odd accessory like a cropped jacket or loose scarf swung around the shoulders. Many women's outfits had large, pointless holes cut in them, and many men's shirts were sheer to the point of being practically transparent. There wasn't much in the name of variety, either. Eden Corp's clothing branch had had a massive influence on the fashion scene of, not just Eden city itself, but a lot of the country. Their style could be described as sleek, stylish and provocative. Not unlike the city itself. Mostly black or white with splashes of bright, saturated colours.

Bear looked down at his own clothes. Grey, brown, loose-fitting, worn. Anybody could take a single glance at him and tell his class. And they did. People didn't seem to want to hide the fact they were staring, even after he made straight eye contact with them.

Spider didn't seem that bothered. Whether he was used to it, didn't notice, or simply didn't care, Bear couldn't be certain.

The fact that people moved away when they passed him didn't bother him, because he didn't much want to be in the way of them, either.

Before long, gradually making their way further away from the inner city, they came across a large, dome-shaped, glass building with its own plaza built around it. The vacuum-train station. The plaza itself was decorated with water features and tourist information boards, flashing out advertisements and proclamations about how flawless and majestic the city was. From the wide open space, the sky was visible, and the sun beamed down through gathering clouds in such a way that it felt blinding after years of the grim darkness sealed away. And here on the vac-train plaza, they stopped.

There were considerably less people here on the plaza, a relief from the feeling of being trapped in a swarm of pedestrians on the narrow pavements.

Bear stood to face a tall billboard and found himself rather drawn-in to its advertisements. The shiny new fashions it was showing were a whole lot different to the 'inspirational' messages that the inner city put up on its boards for its less fortunate residents.

Before long, the picture changed to something else. A news page announcing that some supposedly popular celebrity was spotted wearing the same outfit twice (shock horror), alongside the tidings that there had been an inexplicable rise in infant mortality rates as of late. Bear could not understand how these two subjects seemed so equal in importance to the masses that they could share a billboard.

"Not to be... 'elitist', or anything..." started a man's voice a few metres away to the right, "But if those people who live in the inner city hate it so much, like, why don't they just work harder? Then they could afford to get out of that tip."

"I know right, like how hard can it be to just do some honest work for once?"

Bear's head turned to see who was speaking, and both the man and the woman he had been talking to turned to stare him right in the eye with a tangible air of contempt. They looked him up and down with no shame before looking back to each other and walking off so they weren't in his vicinity. Their conversation had probably been sparked by the sight of him and Spider.

Spider, who had been consulting with an interactive map until now, snaked up behind as he adjusted the belt on his hips.

"Ready?" he asked, cheerily, but his face fell when Bear didn't look back to him, "Is something up?"

Bear cleared his throat and looked down to Spider, averting his eyes from the couple who were still in view,

"N-no, I'm fine, let's go," he replied, but his tone was not an assuring one.

"The office is just along this way," Spider continued, beginning to lead the way down the road.

Bear followed closely, stooping slightly, and suddenly feeling – despite the six-foot-five to his height – very small.

The building itself was a lofty but narrow, dull grey box set between two apartment blocks. Its pointed roof sat upon four storeys and the arch above the frosted glass double doors announced the name of the establishment: Canis Lupus Child Placement. The wolf head logo underneath showed this was a reference to the lupine animal family and not the skin condition.

By the time Bear and Spider had arrived at the door, the rain had started to fall quite heavily. Bear's hair was practically black from the wet and his nose had turned a flushed red. The decision to not wear a jumper had been a detrimental one.

Spider's hood, he had found, had a hole in it, but the mask over his mouth and nose was keeping his face warm enough at least. He stared up at the tall doors, wondering why they hadn't just gone inside yet.

As he wrung his hands, Bear mentally prepared himself for what he'd face inside this building. The judgemental stare of tired social workers and people in formal-wear, perhaps. A look of fake sympathy upon this poor, soaking young man. Or would there be a look of fear meeting his eyes as the people inside observed his height and broad-shouldered frame. Whatever was waiting for him inside, he decided, he'd come all this way – through biting cold and a foul hotel and one set of rather sharp Rottweiler teeth – for his little brother, and he wasn't about to give up now.

"Hey," Spider stopped him as he stepped forward to approach the doors, "I guess this is goodbye, then?"

"...What? Why do you say that?"

"Well I did what I said. I said I'd take you as far as the offices. Here we are. Ciao, auf wiedersehen, all that?"

"I… Well, at least wait inside, Spider. Get dried off a bit. I mean it's not like I'm never going to see you again... Right?"

Spider shrugged. And although he was still very much a mystery, as he stood there with the front of his hair flopped down over his eye like some pathetic wet tendril, Bear couldn't say he didn't feel pity for him.

"Come inside, I want you to wait until I've spoken to whoever's in there."

"If you say so."

Bear pushed open the doors, decisively, and stepped into a long, shiny, sterile-looking lobby. The floor was pure white, as were the walls, and the only furniture were a few black, modern-art-style chairs that didn't look very comfy. Then there was only the reception desk at the end of the room, behind which sat a woman with a rather impressive oversized cravat. She did not raise her gaze until Bear approached the desk, his wet shoes squeaking on the floor as he went.

When she did make eye contact, there was an expression on her face that said she knew he was from the inner city, didn't expect him to have an IQ above maybe ten, but was also quite intimidated by the fact he looked like he would be able to pick her up and throw her out of the window in one move.

"Can I help you?" she started.

"Yeah, have you… uh..." Bear stuttered, suddenly unaware of what he was supposed to say, "Do you know anything about what happened with a kid called Ambrose Orson?"

"Depends who's asking," the woman replied, flatly.

"Family. Estranged."

This explanation didn't seem satisfactory as there was no response.

"Please," Bear sighed, "I'm just trying to find my brother."

The woman chewed the inside of her cheek in thought. She clearly didn't trust Bear much, not least because of his societal standing, but she wheeled her chair around to face the thin screen on her left.

"Name."

"Be-… *Barret* Orson."

It was clear the display was showing Bear's entire history and possibly personality. Eden kept information on all its workers, and inhabitants who were born or educated in the city. There probably wasn't a resident in its boundaries without an extensive file.

"'Barret Orson. Born two-thousand-and-fifty-eight. Parents… April and Wilton Orson… spouse… none… occupation'…" here the woman paused to look at Bear out of the corner of her eye, "…'Unemployed'." she finished with disdain.

"Yes," Bear nodded, swallowing, a sudden feeling of shame washing over him, "That's me. Can you tell me where my brother is?"

"I'm sorry, that's confidential."

"But I'm… *family*. I have ID on me, I can prove it."

The woman looked directly up at him, and though her face was angled upwards she still seemed to be staring down her nose. With a vague gesture, she gave the impression that she would like to view the ID in question. Clearly being bothered by somebody from the belly of the city wasn't something she enjoyed, and she wasn't shy about making it evident.

Bear rummaged around in his bag, fishing about for his identity card. His hand brushed past Ambrose's old teddy at the bottom and as his fingers met with its fur, a strange feeling filled his stomach, as if this was a reminder that his brother really was out there somewhere and not just something he had dreamed up.

He pulled out the card, now mildly shaken, and presented it to the receptionist, who regarded it intently. Eventually, she handed it back.

"I'm assuming you want custody of the child."

"Ultimately. I'd… like to visit first. Ideally."

"…He's with a family by the name of Whittaker. They live in Chester," she said, taking a scrap piece of paper and scribbling down a short address, "You'll have to appeal to the court if you want third party custody. If you know what that is."

"Chester?" Bear repeated, in a sort of stunned disbelief, discarding the latter half of what he'd been told. Chester was the sort of place you only lived in nowadays if you had enough money to purchase a TV that takes up an entire wall. It was not the sort of place that Bear expected a poor child from central Eden would be sent for foster care. It was also an hour's drive away and Bear had no car.

"How am I supposed to get to *Chester?*"

"Take the train or something," the receptionist sighed, "Look, I've told you where your brother is, I can't help you any more. I have other jobs to get to."

Bear didn't reply to her short, impatient statement, but he got his bag together and breathed out a half-hearted 'thank you' before turning away.

His stride was stopped short when he noticed that Spider was nowhere to be seen.

Cautiously, he made his way to the door, which slid open for him as he approached. Still the rain poured down, even heavier now, drops spattering Bear's nose and catching in his eyelashes.

"Spider?" he called, peering through the rain for any sign of the elusive eccentric, "Spider!"

After shaking his head, spraying water everywhere within in a three-foot circumference, he crossed the road to where his his eyes had settled on a small figure facing a street lamp.

"Spider?"

"Oh- hi. I didn't think you'd mind if I just. Stepped outside."

"What are you doing out here?"

Spider looked back to the pole of the street lamp momentarily. A missing persons poster was stuck up on its surface, reading out – under a photo of the unfortunate soul, water-smudged beyond recognition – a name: Nicodemo Lazarus Runo.

"Nothing," Spider replied, shortly, "How did it go?"

"Well I have good news and bad news."

"I'll take the good news."

"We know where Ambrose is."

Spider's face broke out into a grin, although his mouth was kept hidden by his mask.

"Well that's *great*!" he chirped, enthusiastically, rolling the 'r'. In his eyes was a genuine relief and excitement, a glint of actual warmth. But his expression swiftly fell, and his gaze turned wary, "...What's the bad news?"

"He's in foster care with a family in Chester," Bear replied with a grim look.

"...So? Let's go to Chester."

"Spider, I don't have the money to get to Chester and back."

Spider stared up to him with those sharp, keen eyes and stayed silent for quite a good while. He seemed to be thinking deeply, as was normal for him.

"There's a buy-and-sell shop I know, back in the city centre," he told Bear, eventually, "We could sell something there."

"Like what? I don't really have anything of value here."

Spider raised his arm to show the grappling hook device strapped to his arm. His *prized* grappling hook.

Ever since Bear had met him, he'd kept this device in tip top shape. Cleaned it every time he was at Marcus and Leyland's flat. In fact he'd only ever taken it off to clean, as far as Bear knew. It let him scale the buildings to get off the ground; up high on the rooftops where it was safe. Where he could sit and watch over the city, and sleep at night in relative peace. He'd fished the thing out of a massive bin, he'd said. Not really bothered about where it came from. His best find yet, he'd proclaimed.

"Oh- Spider... *no. No!*" Bear sighed, a wave of guilt crashing over him as he ran one of his large hands over his face, "I can't let you do that. You *love* that thing."

"It's just a thing."

"But it's *yours*. I'm not taking advantage of one of the only things you own."

"Bear, I know how it feels to not have anything. When I woke up that time… I had nothing but the clothes on my back. I survived for months before I found th-"

A large van rolled past, its tyres colliding with a deep puddle that sent a wave over the pavement, drenching Spider's entire right hand side. He shook himself off in vain, looking a bit wet and pathetic.

"...What I'm saying is," he continued, "I don't need this thing to keep me going. But you need your brother."

Bear didn't want to say it, but he had to admit that this was correct. He hated to accept charity, especially from *Spider* of all people, who didn't have a thing to his name aside from his clothes, his grappling hook and the contents of his utility belt (which consisted of not much more than some first aid supplies, things he'd found on the floor and a half-empty tin of Altoids).

"Let me help. Don't feel bad."

With another sigh and a guilty smile, Bear uttered a small 'come on then...' and turned in the direction they'd initially come from.

"I must owe you… at *least* two sandwiches by now or something."

"*Hmm...*" Spider droned, "Make it three."

"You didn't have to do this for me, you know."

"And what, leave you to walk to Chester?" scoffed Spider as he made himself comfortable in his seat.

"Well… No… I'm sure I could have scraped together some cash somehow. I feel guilty that you sold your stuff."

"Too late!"

They sat with backs against the window, on the two seats which bore the least suspicious stains. This was a budget bus line, and the chairs were not easily wipeable. The old, flat fabric upon the seat was marked with traces from previous passengers, whether that be spilled drink, burnt holes or a mysteriously sticky patch. Whatever it was, Spider had seen worse, and as much as he hated to admit it, Bear had, too, back in the Arcady hotel.

The whole vehicle smelled of sweat, ammonia, cheap cleaning fluid and some chips that had been chewed up and spat out. In fact, if he craned his neck to look under the opposite seats, Spider could just about see an unidentifiable substance that may have been the source of one of the wondrous aromas aboard the bus. Still, it was brighter and less suspicious than most of the jitneys and pirate cabs that operated inside Eden.

"Hey," he smiled eventually, "Look what I got!" and he excitedly flapped a little pamphlet in Bear's face.

"Some paper?"

"I picked it up at the station. It's about Chester. Things to see."

"We're not… tourists. You do realise that, don't you?"

"At least see what it's like. Where Ambrose is living... Look, there's a museum! I've never been to a museum… I don't think..."

"Spider-"

"Or a… clock. We could see the clock..."

Bear looked momentarily at the pamphlet but was distracted quickly by Spider's previous words. He always teetered on the edge of 'should I' and 'shouldn't I' regarding asking questions, especially about Spider's past. Or lack thereof. But curiosity overrode the sense of wariness in this case.

"What's it like? Not knowing, I mean," he inquired, as quietly and politely as he could.

"...About museums?"

"No, I mean, just in general. About yourself."

"Well. I don't mind it. I like to make up theories."

"About who you were?"

Spider nodded, still regarding the leaflet in his hands with a measure of interest.

"I could have been a doctor! Or a criminal. I could have been a psychologist. Or an assassin. Man, I could have had a wife. I might have been someone's brother, someone's hero, who knows?"

"You ever wonder if you have family? And where they are?"

"Naturally. But I like to imagine they were nice. And I can do that. I can imagine. And it doesn't matter if I'm right or not."

"So if there were a possibility you could remember everything, would you try to find answers?"

"Who says I haven't tried?"

"Well, I-"

"I think I like to believe that I was a good person. I don't know what I would do if I found out I wasn't. Do you think I'm a good person, Bear?"

Bear paused for a second. The whining and puffing of vehicular workings filled the otherwise silent bus. Then nothing as they slowed to a stop to pick up passengers (who sat as far away from the Eden folk as they could). Still nobody spoke a word.

Ever since he'd first met Spider, Bear had never been able to put his finger on whether he was friend material or not. On one hand, he could be anybody. He could even be pretending to have amnesia as a disguise to mask the truth… whatever that truth was. But after all that he had done – defending Bear against the dog, helping him find a hotel and locating Canis Lupus, and now selling one of his few belongings to be able to afford this very journey – it was hard to believe that he had anything but good intentions. Even despite what

Spitfire, AKA Leyland, said. So Bear made up his mind on the matter of trust, finally, because if there was anything else that Spider could have done to prove himself, Bear couldn't think of it.

"Yes, Spider," he said, with a firm nod, "I think you are a very good person."

Spider's face broke into a content smile, like his payment for all he'd done was simply being trusted and he was perfectly happy with that.

"Thank you, Bear," He replied, sincerely, "I hope you're right."

As the bus rolled out of the city, the towering buildings gradually turned to smaller ones until there were no buildings at all. Eden was behind, in the rear window, and Bear did not care to turn his neck and look back. The grime was replaced, in due course, with a patchwork of fields in every shade of green from shamrock to chartreuse.

Astounded, Bear slowly rose from his seat. Using the handles hanging from the roof to steady himself, he stepped over to gaze out of the window in astonishment.

For as far as the eye could see, there was this wondrous green. A deep, dark juniper in the trees, a lighter sample for the bushes and grasses. Bear had only seen these shades in art, or in photographs he assumed had been faked or manipulated in some way. It had never occurred to him that he might one day be able to see them with his own two eyes. He didn't even notice the dull motorway they were travelling on, the noise of the other cars passing them, or the stench inside the bus. Or the specks of grey – other towns and cities splattered at random in the distance.

"So that's it, is it?" he breathed, "That's what's out there?"

He couldn't really wrap his head around the emptiness, the potential, the space. Or, even, why anybody would leave it to move to the backward, forlorn rat trap of Eden City.

"It's bigger than you think," Spider said, simply, "Or so I've heard."

"I feel..." Bear started, but then gave up. Articulating his emotions to Spider always felt like a waste of time, as it was rare that a response would be given. Despite the frankly thoughtful things that he came out with sometimes, Spider was still primarily a creature of few words.

Managing to tear his eyes away from the rolling green expanse beyond – a blank canvas of possibility as far as he was concerned – Bear looked back to Spider, who had not spoken a word in a good few minutes.

Instead of focusing on his little pamphlet, as Bear had expected, Spider was transfixed by the sights outside the window. His gaze was set, unblinking, far into the distance. He did not smile, but Bear could swear there was a sparkle of wonder in his sleepy eyes.

There was, at first, an apprehensive air about stepping off the bus and into a new city. Bear hadn't left Eden for his entire life, and as far as he knew, neither had Spider. The bus was just an extension of that place, the rotten smells and the grime stayed with the vehicle, as if you'd never left Eden at all. Even after a transfer or two, when the buses got marginally cleaner. But when he left the last bus, Bear knew, that would be it – a brand new location. And he hated to admit it, but he was terrified.

As accursed as Eden was, it was still home.

But the buildings looked different here. Shorter, built with lighter bricks. The first building outside the bus interchange had a grey sloping roof atop its three storeys, it appeared to be an apartment complex. Unlike the old Orson residence, it looked rather pleasant. The windows were clean and there was even a hedge in the trough planter under the front windows. A well-kept one at that.

Cautiously, both Bear and Spider stepped out onto the ground at last. The bus interchange was a large, open-air place, with the hissing of hydraulic brakes and the commotion of commuters all around.

Bear was suddenly uncomfortably aware of the stink he had carried with him from Eden. The air didn't mask it any more. The stench of smog and wet cardboard and ammonia was no longer present, instead the breeze carried a whiff of petrol from the buses and a salty smell of fish and chips from a man walking past with a styrofoam container in his hands. The only foul odour, Bear knew, was himself, and he knew it thanks to the disgusted faces of the people who walked past him. They walked faster.

He lifted the hem of his top up to his nose and sniffed gently, just to make sure he wasn't imagining it. And he wasn't.

Immediately his nose was met with a pungent odour of damp, sweat and dry vomit. Not smells that had come from his own neglect of hygiene – he'd always made sure he was clean – but simply smells that lingered in Eden, and lingered on him, on his skin,

in his hair, in the back of his throat. And he felt even more ashamed
than he had done when the rich folk had looked down their noses at
him in the Magenta District.

Slowly, Bear smoothed the fabric back down over his skin,
and his hand lingered there over his stomach as he nervously gazed
about the place.

Spider hadn't spoken a word yet, but the sounds of him
cracking his knuckles and fiddling with his belt evidenced that he
was not as stunned as Bear was by this change in scenery.

"You have the address, right?"

"Y...Yeah..." Bear nodded, pulling himself out of the trance
that had frozen him, "Right here..." and he took the scrap paper out
of his pocket.

After entering the location into his phone, he and Spider
noticed that it was but a half hour walk from their current location.

"Eat before we go?" Spider suggested, clearly having been
enticed by the waft of fish and chips.

"Where?"

"I'm sure we can find somewhere."

Bear had to admit he felt reluctant. Not only was he
concerned that the smell he had carried with him would disgust other
customers, but the trip had given him a nervous stomach.
Nevertheless, he could tell that Spider was feeling peckish, and after
he'd sold his grappling hook it was the least Bear could do to let him
find a takeaway somewhere.

It was within an hour that both of the city visitors had
located the Roman amphitheatre and settled down there against one
of the stone walls. Behind them, on the surface, was a lush patch of
green grass that made up the semicircle surrounding the
amphitheatre. And on the other side of the flat wall, a small car park
decorated with the odd tree. It was different from the Magenta
District in Eden, less industrial, luxurious in another sort of way. The

shorter, but more decorated buildings surrounding, the smaller roads with grass verges, the relative quiet of sitting in this stone semicircle. In a way, it was even nicer than where people worked their entire lives to get to in Eden.

"So..." Bear started as he licked his fingers of the salt from his last meal, "What was an 'amphitheatre' for?"

Spider took this as a spectacular opportunity to consult his little leaflet, and so blossomed it with a flourish.

"...'For events such as gladiator battles, animal killing and executions'," he rolled, proudly, despite Bear's disturbed look, "This place would have been *huge*. Once upon a time. Here. Look at the drawing."

Bear took a quick look at the illustration but then turned away, finding the idea of animal battles a little jarring. He wondered momentarily whether there had been any bears in the arena, and how he might have fared fighting against one.

He thought back to the dog attack behind the butcher's and decided that he would, in fact, not fare very well.

"Whaddya' gonna' do, Bear?" Spider hummed, still engrossed in his tourist guide.

"What do you mean?"

"When we get there. Where are you taking him after?"

"To… to the housing I found. It's like a shelter, for people who don't have homes. And then they find you a permanent home somewhere."

"How are you going to pay for rent?"

"...I'll get a job somewhere."

Spider looked at him from the corner of his eye, sceptically.

"I'll cross that bridge when I come to it, alright?"

"Alright."

Bear gazed up at the darkening sky, as the sun began to set. It almost didn't feel real, being in such a different place. Usually, looking up from outside, Bear could only see a web of wires and washing lines strung up about the buildings, blocking the view. But now, the sky had this wonderful mishmash of colour, all blue and pink and orange, with clouds that looked like sheep's wool.

Maybe he had been injured worse than he thought back behind the butcher's, and this was all a creation of his imagination that he had made as he lay in a coma in a hospital bed somewhere.

As he thought about the incident, his leg began to pulsate with a burning pain again and his hand shot down subconsciously to grasp it.

"We really ought to get you to hospital, Bear," Spider observed, now considerably less cheery-sounding, "You look really pale and blotchy."

"I'm fine," Bear insisted, "Really, it's just sore."

"I want you to go to a hospital. Do it after you find Ambrose if you must. But go."

Bear was mildly thrown by Spider being so direct, as opposed to his usual more timid manner. He reluctantly agreed to go to an urgent treatment centre at the first chance he got.

"It's too late to get to the house before nightfall, isn't it?"

"I think so, Bear. I think so..."

"Where do we go for the night?"

Spider shrugged,

"This seems as good a place as any to me," he said.

Bear looked at him, a little uncomfortable with the idea of sleeping outside.

"Is that what you did in Eden? Is that what you meant… when you said you 'have places'? You just kip out on the street, in the open?" He asked, visibly concerned.

"I had nothing to lose," Spider replied, casually, shuffling around to sit more comfortably, "I mean, with Spitfire being the way he is, I didn't much fancy sleeping in the same building as him."

"Should have called himself Spite-fire."

Spider knocked his head back with an unexpected cackle. Clearly he hadn't been expecting a joke, of all things, to come from Bear. When he'd recovered from this, he put his hands behind his head and continued, "When you're in a position like mine… you can afford to take risks. Listen, you get some sleep. I'll stay awake and keep guard. If that makes you feel any better?"

"Are you sure?"

"*Surrre.* Don't worry about it. I'm not even tired. We could even do shifts."

"*Shifts...*" Bear smiled with a gentle chuckle.

They were both silent for a while, watching the traffic rumble past and breathing the semi-clear air. Despite being in a very unfamiliar place, Bear could breathe easy. He didn't feel in danger here, didn't feel like he'd get ripped to shreds if he looked at someone the wrong way, and didn't feel like he'd get food poisoning from the chips he just ate. So regardless of the unsure outcome of his adventure, he decided it had been worth it at least to feel this way.

"Hey, Spider?"

"Yeah?"

"I think that, under other circumstances, this whole trip... it would have been very fun."

"I think so, too."

"I'm glad you came flying through Marcus' window that one time."

"I am, too. Very glad."

"I don't think Marcus was, though."

"I'll dodge the table next time."

"So… this is it."

"Are you *sure* this is the right house?"

"It's the address you wrote down, isn't it?"

"…Yeah…"

"Then it's the right house."

Bear looked back up to the tiny quaint terrace in front of him and wrung his hands, nervously. He wasn't sure what he had been expecting, but somehow he still felt surprised.

A mahogany brown UPVC door stood in front of him, complete with rusty postbox and the number one-hundred-and-four. The blinds in the windows were down, slats flattened to hide any view into the front room. A small ornamental husky dog was placed on the sill, one side faded from the sun shining on it over the years. Despite being extraordinarily small, the patch of soil at the front of the house was very well kept, decorated with a couple of evergreen bushes, and roses which were currently nothing but thick stems spotted with thorns.

"Well? Knock!" Spider urged.

Bear cast one last glance down the street; the red brick houses seemed to stretch on into eternity. In fact, the only reason he couldn't see *more* houses was that the street curved out of view.

Swallowing his fear, Bear stepped forward to unlatch the little black iron gate, although he could have easily stepped over the wall. It emitted a screech as the bottom dragged over the flagstones and the hinges protested their use.

"I'll… Wait around at the end of the street," Spider told him. He clearly assumed the street *had* an end at some point, which Bear still disbelieved. So off he tootled, way down the road, where he would no doubt get bored after a while and wander off.

Gingerly, Bear approached the door, his heart thundering in his chest. What or who would he be met with? Would he even be allowed to see his brother? Gathering his thoughts, he knocked.

At the sound, a dog began to bark behind the door. From the window decoration, Bear guessed this was a husky. Still, the sound alone made his heart speed up even more, reminding him of the attack behind the butcher's once more. This didn't help his already shallow breathing. However, he attempted to remain calm and collected, masking the beating of his heart by rubbing circles in his chest.

Spider had a few good qualities. He was agile, he could fairly accurately judge someone's character by a short conversation and he could problem-solve in a flash to get out of a sticky situation. However, staying focused was *not* a quality he possessed. He had a nasty habit of getting distracted with the smallest possible thing and trailing off into goodness knows what territory. Today was no different, and despite wanting to stand and wait for Bear like he'd said, the sight of a newspaper A-board outside a corner store was too strong a temptation to resist.

Telling himself he wouldn't be long, Spider scurried over to get a good look at today's headline. As he read, his face shifted into a tight-lipped frown.

'EdenTech Faces £1M Lawsuit After Selling User Data' announced the article in bold text.

Spider wondered why he hadn't heard anything about this topic when he was back in Eden. He also couldn't help wondering who the data was sold *to* and what they intended to do with it. But as far as he knew, he didn't have a single device, account, password or email, so it wasn't his problem.

Absently, he lifted his eyes to gaze into the shop window at all the delights inside. It was full to the brim with bottles, boxes and bright yellow 'SALE' stickers. A strip light flickered momentarily over the cashier's desk, where a middle aged man with a spectacular beard stood cleaning the surface. He turned, seemingly sensing someone was there, and made eye contact with Spider, pausing mid-wipe. Spider stood, frozen in place, for a good few seconds before turning to leave, wandering a little further along the endless street.

It was quite a journey, and along the way he saw a good many unfamiliar sights. Neatly-kept gardens, pleasant little outdoor ornaments, lampposts free of graffiti or posters, pavement devoid of crumpled, empty cans. A feeling of not belonging lingered around him as he walked, the windows of the houses felt like they were watching him, as if they were VIP boxes looking down on a theatre stage, or huge TV screens monitoring him.

He pulled his hood up over his head and carried on.

The one thing that finally halted him in his tracks was a little old lady with a river of groceries surrounding her feet.

"Hey, lemme help you!" Spider called, his voice stopping the woman half-way through bending over to pick up her shopping.

"Oh, thank you, young man," she said, in that voice that every old woman has, glasses chains swinging gently as she stood straight again, "Nobody stops to help an OAP these days, especially not the youth. All too busy looking at their… whatever flashy gadget people use now. My grandchildren used to come and visit me, but they all moved to the big city. Kids and their dreams, you'll know about that…" she rambled.

Spider was about to inform her that, actually, despite his height, he was not quite a 'youth', but he refrained as he remembered that he didn't actually know that with one-hundred per-cent certainty. Instead he simply crouched down and began to pick up each item one by one and place them in the safety of the little purple folding shopping trolley. He hoped that she didn't think he was too dirty to be handling her newly-purchased belongings, but maybe her old-age senses would dull the smell of him.

As he lifted the last items – two large oranges – and rose to his feet, the pensioner laid a frail hand over his and looked up to him with that kind smile that grannies have.

"You keep them, dear."

"Oh! Oh, are you sure?" Spider asked, a little thrown by being called 'dear' and by the kind offer.

"Think of it as a thank you for helping a little old woman."

"Well, thank you..."

And just like that, the old dear tootled off down the street, trolley rumbling along behind her.

Spider remained there in the road for a second, rolling the oranges around in his hands, before breaking out into a content grin. Cheerily, he set back off towards the direction of Bear, his pace a sunny jog-skip combo. He tried in vain to fit the oranges into his utility belt pockets as he walked, eventually accepting the fact he would have to carry them one in each hand.

It didn't take him long to reach the corner where he had been waiting previously. Just in time, in fact, it seemed, as Bear then rounded the corner to meet him.

"Bear! Bear, look what I got!" Spider chirped, presenting his travelling companion with the two fruits in his hands, "I helped out this old woman and she gave them to me! One for each of us, look! I mean, *yes,* they *have* been on the floor, but that's what the peel is for- ... Bear?"

Bear stared down, despondently, upon the citrus, as if it had just told him some depressing news.

"Oh, maybe you don't like oranges. I should have asked. Do you have an orange allergy, Bear?"

"It's... not that, Spider," Bear sighed with a shake of the head.

"Then what is it?"

"...There was no answer. Nobody came to the door,"

"Oh... *ah, boy...* Uh... We're sure it was the right house, yeah?"

"It was the one I had written down."

"Maybe they're just out? We could check back later."

"What if they've taken a weekend away... we can't afford to stay here and wait for their return."

"We don't know that they've done that-"

"I mean, we came all this way. For nothing? No response? I-"

"*Bear.* Chill. They probably just popped out for bread or something. We'll come back later, yeah?"

"Yeah, I guess..."

"In the meantime, we really ought to get you to a hospital. Hey, that'll take your mind off it."

Bear became suddenly aware of the pain in his leg. Oftentimes, the stress of his expedition took his attention away from it, but every so often he would be reminded of his bandaged limb. He could tell it was getting worse, and so was his head. The dressing hadn't been changed since initially in the Arcady hotel, which probably wasn't helping the state of it. Bear had to admit that an urgent treatment centre sounded like a fair idea.

"That's a good idea."

"I'm sure we'll find Ambrose soon. We're so close, we can't just accept defeat now, can we?"

Bear shook his head and forced a smile.

"Would an orange maybe make you feel better?"

"Yeah," Bear smiled, taking it gratefully, "Thanks, Spider."

"Hey, Spider."

"Hey… how are you feeling?"

"Like trash."

"I'm not surprised."

Spider took a seat beside the hospital bed, putting his feet up on the chair and resting his elbows on his knees as was his habit. The whole room was blindingly white and smelled so pungently of menthol that Spider could feel his sinuses spasm and the inner corners of his eyes begin to water. Never before had his breathing felt so clear, nor so tingly.

"What did they say it was?" he asked, rubbing his nose with his knuckle.

"Some infection. Cellulitis or something… I think. They said it could have turned into sepsis if I'd have left it much longer," Bear replied. He sat up in the bed with one leg up on the mattress and one dangling down to the floor, "Good job you convinced me to come, huh?"

"Spider knows best."

"Spider knows best... Hey look, bud, they're keeping me in for a bit to monitor me. And by a bit I mean like a week. That's why I called you in to talk to you. I can stay here, but you can't. So..."

"I know."

"I think you ought to go back to Eden."

For a second the only sound was the ticking of the clock and the muffled commotion of doctors and nurses going about their jobs out in the hallway.

Spider moved his legs down from the seat and shuffled around a bit. The prospect of going back to the big city wasn't too bad, he was used to being there, after all. But the idea of leaving meek, nervous Bear all alone in an unfamiliar town was less desirable.

"Marcus can take you in again. You'll be safe with him."

"What about you?"

"I'll go back to the house until I get an answer. I'll ask the neighbours, I'll do whatever I need to. And if I never get an answer, I'll head back to Marcus," Bear told him with a weak smile, "Don't worry about me. I'll be fine."

Spider returned his smile, slightly reassured but still doubtful. After all, the last time he'd left Bear alone, he'd gone out and got himself in trouble. Thus landing himself here, in this bed, in this room.

"I guess this is goodbye, then," Spider said with a shrug.

"For now," Bear corrected him, kindly.

"For now."

"This whole trip… I feel like I've grown."

"...But you were already like six foot five-"

"I mean as a *person*, Spider," Bear chuckled, "Thanks for getting me this far. I couldn't have done it without you. I mean it."

"Oh, don't worry, I know," Spider replied, smugly.

"I still owe you those three sandwiches."

"When you get your own place you can mail me them. I like peanut butter ones best, so don't forget."

Bear gave a light laugh, lingering on the concept of him and Ambrose making peanut butter sandwiches. As simple as the mental image was, it still strengthened his resolve to find that kid and get away from here. What Spider had said about needing something to hope for to help you carry on had been right after all.

Slowly, he held out his hand to shake, resolute that this decision was the best one he could make in this instance. When Spider took his hand, he tugged him forwards into a brief hug, giving him a pat on the back that was just a little too forceful for his size.

"I'll see you around, yeah?"

"Hopefully," Spider nodded, rolling his shoulder blades back. He got up from his chair slowly and brushed himself down. Although he'd been on his lonesome as long as he could remember, for at least the past four years, it felt a little odd going off alone again. Still, perhaps it was for the best. If he looked hard enough he might even be able to find another grappling hook. If he hadn't sold his to get here, he could return to his rooftop life no problem. He didn't regret it, though. If he'd done nothing good in his life before, helping Bear find his brother was the one good deed he hoped would overshadow anything he may have done in the past.

"Be… be careful, alright?" Bear swallowed.

"I'll try," Spider smiled back at him, "You be careful, too."

"I will."

"See you, Bear."

"Goodbye, Spider."

The heavy doors gradually eased closed behind Spider as he left the room, leaving him standing in one white corridor in a maze of identical rooms and halls. He stopped off at the bathrooms on his way out to clean himself up. The trek back to Eden would be a long one without company, but Spider was used to it by now. He plucked some travel brochures from a stand by the exit as he left and shoved them in one of his belt pouches, right next to his half-empty Altoid tin. If he spent his time wisely, he might even be able to go see that fancy clock before he got back on the bus.

<u>Chapter 20: Deluge</u>

The trip back was, as expected, almost unbearably quiet. Perhaps even more so than Spider had expected. He wasn't much one for making small talk usually, but after having travelled with Bear for a few days, he'd come to appreciate having a conversational companion at the ready.

Bus people, he found, were not the most talkative. He could swear there was not a single word spoken between any of the other passengers the entire way there. He would have taken a nap, only he had no sure-fire way of making sure he woke up at his stop, so he persevered and stayed awake.

Eden was one of those places that you put up fine with when you're there, but once you leave, you don't want to go back. Rather like a repetitive job, or some old person's house that always has a strange smell.

Spider wasn't exactly thrilled to be back in the place, despite having lived there his entire (known) life. Nor was he excited about going back to Marcus' flat and feeling like a leech. Especially without his grappling hook to get around with. At least then he could have stolen away to spend the night alone in some hideout or other, but now he was pretty much stuck staying with Marcus.

The fact it was raining only made it worse. Making his way through the Magenta district, Spider pulled his hood up against the downpour and heaved a sigh, his breath puffing out like smoke from his mouth. He was used to the rain, but that didn't mean he didn't hate it. If he hurried, he could get back to the flat before he froze.

He walked a fair way, feet splashing up puddles against his legs, a hole in his shoe letting the dirty water soak his soles, before he came to an alley opening where he could slip back into the inner city. Immediately the smell became more pungent and the streets became darker. The corner of a damp newspaper fluttered pathetically in the wind and an empty drinks can (Eden-Nutrition's 'cranberry' pop, Spider had tried it before and it *didn't* taste of cranberries) bounced along the ground before eventually smacking into an upright billboard with a satisfying *clank*.

"Hey!"

Spider raised his head at last to see where the voice had originated from, fluttering the raindrops away from his lashes to try and clear his vision.

"Hey Spider!"

From the left.

Spider turned to the source to find a shadowy figure underneath a canopy, hunched over slightly in the cold. As the character stepped forward, the meagre swash of neon lights trickling in from the Magenta District showed up the faintest of details; a black leather jacket and blonde, green-tipped hair.

"Leyland…"

"He*yyy*..!" Spitfire replied, a little awkwardly, his voice lower and less brash than usual, "Where have you been?"

"Away… What are you doing here?"

"Marcus kicked me out, man. Where else was I gonna go? Hey, I'm glad you're here, I wanna talk to you."

Spider sighed, though in himself felt rather anxious. Just him and the man who tried to poison him, alone in a dark alley. A recipe for disaster, by anyone's standards.

"I don't know what you want, Spitfire, but you won't get it from me."

"I need you to forgive me, yeah? Cause… I think if you do, Marcus will let me back in his flat. We can all be mates again. Look, I'm sorry about the thing. The drink thing. I shouldn't have done it."

"No, you shouldn't have."

"...You're not gonna forgive me, are you?"

"I don't think I could live with you, in the same flat. You tried to kill me," Spider answered, and started to walk away. He was prepared to forgive in his heart, but telling that to Spitfire seemed like it could only end badly. He was a wolf in sheep's clothing right now, and Spider knew it.

For a few paces there was silence, and Spider really began to think he'd escaped the conversation before it could turn sour, but of course it couldn't be that simple.

"YOU DON'T KNOW WHO YOU ARE," Spitfire called after him, *"DO YOU?"*

Spider stopped in his tracks. His recent history with the guy had hinted at their being some more past interaction between them. Spider knew the only people who knew about his memory loss were Bear, and Marcus to a small extent. So unless Marcus had told Spitfire something…

"If you had a chance to remember everything… Would you?"

He still didn't turn back, though the question piqued his interest. It was one he'd asked himself a lot. Even Bear had asked it. He'd answered vaguely then, saying he didn't know what he'd do if he found out he was a bad person. But now, when there seemed to be a chance of actually finding out everything…

"You don't remember me, do you, Spider?"

"No."

Spitfire gave a short '*heh*' of a laugh, moving forward again.

"It's me, man. Your old buddy. You really don't remember?"

"I… don't remember anything."

"We met when we were kids. Your momma knew mine, we lived close. We used to play together all the time, I had those action figures, yeah? You always wanted to be Spiderman..."

Spider swallowed, feeling his arms begin to shake. Despite willing his body to walk away, he found himself glued to the spot, curiosity overwhelming the drive to move.

"I was Superman and you were Spiderman. You ever stopped to think why you were so good with that grappling hook? Cause you watched your hero do stuff like that all the time. Where is that thing, anyway? It's not on your arm."

Still, Spider remained silent.

"We can be buds again, you know," Spitfire continued with a shrug, "It wouldn't be hard. You agree to bury the spanner-"

"Hatchet"

"Right. And I tell you everything. How does that sound?"

"How do I know you're not just making this all up?" Spider asked, sharply, as the rain dripped off his nose and his lips started to go numb.

"Would I lie to you?"

"You tried to kill me. Why?"

Spitfire paused, stuffing his hands in his pockets,

"I was scared, man..."

"Scared?"

"Boy, you really don't remember a thing. I thought you'd want revenge or something..."

"For what?"

"I'll tell you… *if* you help me get back on good terms with my mate Marcus. You're the only one who can help me, the guy hates me now, thinks I'm out for blood, but that's not it. I'm out on the streets, I spent three nights at a place called the Arcady, I think I got fleas now. Plus I got the cops on my tail, thinking I'm some potential murderer or whatever."

Spider finally broke out of his trance and shook himself off, walking away once more. He felt bad, he had to admit, and his curiosity was killing him, but he just couldn't trust Leyland. Not after what he'd done.

"Spider isn't your name, Spider. It's who you wanted to be. Do you want to know your real name? I can tell you!" Spitfire called out, but his words had no effect, "Hey, I've spoken to your momma, she's worried about you, she thinks you're missing! Hey!"

Spider picked up his pace, hoping that he could simply walk away, but the sound of footsteps behind him shattered that idea. There was a false friendliness in Spitfire's voice that masked the true selfish intentions underneath, and his voice only became more insistent and rash as he went on.

"Hey, you might think you're the one who has it bad, but I lost everything, too, you know! Because of you! I thought you'd remember some day; you'd remember what happened! I had to change who I was, man, I had to keep moving, just in case *you* remembered and wanted your own back! Well not any more!"

Breaking out into a run, Spider decided he didn't want to hear it. He plugged his ears with his fingers to block out the noise so that the only things he could hear was the blood pumping in his head and the thumping of his own feet as he ran.

"You're making a bad decision here! Hey! Talk to me, idiot!"

Still no reply. Not a single word. Spider didn't want to think about what he'd be getting himself into if he answered, so he didn't, he just ran.

"You ruined my LIFE, Nico!" Spitfire shouted after him. His leg twisted underneath him, forcing him to stumble to a stop. Exhausted and infuriated, he spat out one last sentence, *"You RUINED it!"*

But Spider didn't hear a word he said.

It had been ten whole days since Bear parted ways with his enigmatic travelling companion, and now he found himself alone once more in an unfamiliar city.

His hospital stay had been pleasant, he'd had a lot of time to think while he healed. Mostly about Ambrose, and where they would go from here. If he managed to get custody, which wasn't even definite yet, the prospect of going out and finding that sheltered housing he'd been aiming for seemed intimidating. Nevertheless, now freed from hospital bed, disinfectant and bandages, Bear carried on with his journey to locate his little brother.

His leg felt a lot better. It no longer burned and stung, although some scarring still remained. Walking didn't hurt like it used to. And he'd cleaned up a lot, too. He looked and smelt a lot better than he had done. A fresh start, that's what it was. The only thing Bear didn't have was money; all he had was about a tenner left over from Spider's grappling hook sale. Still, since the only food he had was what he'd saved from the hospital, he had decided to pop into the nearest supermarket to pick up some water and maybe a treat for Ambrose.

As it turned out, the nearest store was a mere fifteen minute walk away, which was just enough to work out his leg without it hurting too much. Now he knelt in the middle of an aisle, looking at sale labels. He'd feel awful turning up to see his little brother empty-handed.

Slowly, he rose to his feet with a sigh. In the aisle behind the shelf he was facing, he heard a soft-spoken parent tell her child he was allowed to pick out one treat. Bear couldn't remember an instance where he was allowed to pick out a treat as a kid; maybe that's why he was having so much trouble deciding now. *Would a Milky Way bar be sufficient, or might a bag of Revels last longer?*

Light footsteps came merrily around the corner, and with no warning, a small child collided with the side of Bear's right leg.

"Sorry-"

"It's OK, kid-..."

Recognising the voice, Bear glanced down to the right to be met with a familiar soft, hopeful stare.

"Ambrose!"

He fell to his knees, bag slipping off his shoulder and hitting the ground as he did, and wrapped his arms around the kid in relief. For whatever reason, he couldn't close his eyes, just stared ahead at the white supermarket flooring. He didn't question where Ambrose came from, nor why he was here, only relished the relief that his journey hadn't all been in vain. As he breathed into the fabric of his brother's coat, Bear noted that the smell it had was markedly different than usual. Fresher, cleaner, instead of that old damp smell the flat always had.

Slowly, maybe even a little shakily, Bear released his grip on the child.

"I've been looking all over for you," he breathed, quickly rubbing a tear from his eye with his knuckle, "What... what *happened*?"

Ambrose stared back at him, mocha eyes wide in surprise still.

"I... I don't know. It's gone really fast..." he started, quietly.

"Where are mum and dad?"

"I'm not sure. I think they're in jail? Some police people came and took them away, then they helped me pack my stuff and took me to this place... can... can something."

"Canis Lupus?"

"Yeah, I think so. I stayed there for a little bit and a nice doctor lady made sure there was nothing wrong with me. Then they took me here to stay with my new foster parents-"

"What are they like? Do they take care of you? You happy with them? Cause I was thinking we could get out of here. And I mean *out* out-"

Bear paused as he noticed Ambrose's stupefied expression. He sighed and ran a hand over his own flustered face, attempting to compose himself.

"Sorry… I'm sorry," he apologised, "I've just been so worried about you. A...are you okay?"

Ambrose finally smiled, contently.

"I'm okay. I was scared at first. And I was really nervous about meeting my foster parents. But they're really nice. The lady is called Janine and her husband's name is Lucien. And they have a dog! His name is Rhubarb and he's very friendly," here his smile melted off and he instead gazed across at his big brother with a calm solemnity, "...I was worried about you, too, Bear."

Bear cracked a smile in return. An attempt to be of assurance. He didn't want to worry Ambrose with all the details of his trip; staying in the Arcady, getting bitten, sleeping outdoors one night, his stay in hospital. So he didn't mention a word of it.

"I brought something for you!" he breathed with a kind grin on his face before rummaging around in his bag for the old teddy bear he'd been carrying with him this whole time, "Look who it is!"

Ambrose gently took the bear from his brother's hands, face breaking out into a beam of a smile as he held it to his chest. Reunited at last.

"He kept me company on my travels," Bear smiled, peacefully, "I made a friend, too. He helped me get here."

"Where is he?"

"...Back in Eden. But maybe you can meet him one day. Look, buddy, I came to get you, I can get custody, there's this housing place where we can go, just the two of us. We'll get away from that sorry excuse of a city and we'll never have to see another rotten apartment building again. What do you say? No parents, no foster parents, just us."

"You can do that?"

"Sure. I'll need a job but I'm sure that'll be easy enough, I could work in a shop or something. It'd be rough at first but, hey, we'd... manage."

Bear paused, thinking about how he only just scraped by paying rent to Marcus with his savings, how he hadn't been able to find work that suited him and probably would have been out of the flat after a while when his funds ran dry. Would that be what would happen again..?

Before Ambrose could reply, there came the rattly sound of trolley wheels rolling on the floor.

"Oh!"

Bear looked up to the source of the noise and found a short, kind-looking woman with cornrows at the end of the aisle.

"Barret, is it?"

Bear nodded, piecing together in his head that this must be Janine, Ambrose's new foster mother. Wobbling, he got to his feet as she approached. At full height, he towered over her like a burly yet gentle giant.

"Ambrose has told us a lot about you… all good, 'course," Janine carried on, looking a tiny bit intimidated, "Have you had a rough journey?"

"It was… alright," Bear replied, not wishing to disclose the full story with its turmoil.

"Are you going somewhere in particular after this?"

"...No."

"How would you like to come back to our house and have some coffee? It'd be nice for Ambrose to spend some more time with you. You'll have to tell us more about what it's like living in Eden, too. If that's alright with you, of course."

Bear fell silent, rather taken-aback by the gesture. He'd expected the new parents to be a bit opposed to his presence, maybe looking down on him because of where he came from, or his appearance, *anything*. The real outcome was very much on the contrary. And Bear felt pretty confident that the kindly couple would take good care of his little brother.

<u>Chapter 22: Spider and I</u>

"Spider."

"Marcus."

"How are you doing, man?"

Spider stared out over the city below him, crawling with the same life it had always had. Even though Spider had been away, when he came back, nothing had changed. It almost felt like he'd never left at all. Without Bear around, it even felt slightly like he'd just been a figment of Spider's imagination. He wondered how his friend was getting on, wherever he was.

"I'm alright," he said, nodding his head slowly. And he was telling the truth. Despite his return to Eden being a necessary evil, the place *was* home. He'd lived here as far back as he could remember, and it had a sort of strange comfort. Even after seeing the stretching fields outside, Spider was pretty willing to accept that the rest of his life would take place here, too.

Marcus sat down beside him on the rooftop. It was just them now, without Bear or Spitfire. Since Spider's return, the stay in Marcus' flat had been almost completely silent. Neither of them talked much on the regular, but it seemed Marcus was making an effort to spark a conversation now, which Spider appreciated.

"I brought you a cola."

"Oh- thanks..!" Spider smiled, accepting the biting cold can. Up here on the roof, the crack and fizz of opening a drink was the loudest noise around, "...Hey Marcus. There's something I keep meaning to tell you."

"Yeah?"

"When I was coming back from the bus stop the other day… I ran into Leyland."

"I see. Did he talk to you?"

"Yeah. He started going on about my memory. Or lack of it. He told me that we used to be friends when we were kids. Best friends, even. He told me he'd tell me who I am if I… teamed up with him, I guess."

“And?”

Spider shuffled around in the spot he was sitting in and took a little sip of cola.

“Well, I don’t know if anything he told me was true, obviously. How am I to know if he’s making it all up or not? He could be telling me anything.”

“That’s true.”

“And I thought, if I *did* want to know who I was… I wouldn’t want to hear it from him. You know?”

Marcus nodded, thoughtfully. He may not have gone through the same, or even a similar, experience in his life, but it seemed he still understood. If nothing else, he was a great listener.

“So what’ll you do now?” he asked, gently, as Spider absent-mindedly gazed upon his arm – bare of the grappling hook that had aided him so much.

“I dunno…” he breathed with a shrug, “Stick my head in some bins and see if I can find another grappling hook, I guess,” and he cracked a smile.

“You know it’s no trouble having you around the flat. Don’t think you’re leeching off of me or whatever, ‘cause you’re not,” Marcus told him with a note of serious concern in his voice, “You might want to go off adventuring in this city and all, but if you ever find yourself in a jam, there’s always a place for you here.”

Spider’s smile widened into a more genuine, relieved one.

“Home base?”

“Yeah, like that.”

“Thanks, Marcus.”

Spider wasn’t sure he’d ever really thought of a place as home before. He’d always considered the flat a temporary dwelling, like a really casual hotel where he could come and go as he pleased. But the knowledge that he could return here any time he wanted and not have to feel like a burden filled a certain void in his heart. Though unsure of what exactly he’d do next or how he’d go about it, Spider closed his eyes and sat back to enjoy the moment of peace. If he had done nothing good in his life before, helping Bear was enough to convince him he'd done enough to justify his existence, and perhaps solidify his hope that he was a good person.

The sound of a knock at the door rattled through the apartment, audible from the rooftop.

"I'll get it," Spider offered, picking himself up and making his way down the ladder to the balcony, cola can still in hand.

The knock came again.

"Yeah, yeah I'm coming!" Spider called with a sigh as he made his way down the short staircase to the front door. He opened it with exaggerated effort. And as he did, his eyes drifted up the figure in front of him to his face.

"Bear?"

Bear gave a nervous smile down to his, much shorter, friend. In his hands he held the same bag he always did and his face looked to glow with a sort of refreshed vigour.

"Hey, Spider," he said, still rather nervous, "How have you been?"

"Did you find Ambrose?" Spider asked him, completely ignoring the question, concerned to know the reason for his return.

"I did," Bear nodded, "He's living with a nice couple with a dog. They invited me round for tea. Did you know that there's over twenty-thousand types of tea in the world, Spider? They were telling me all about it."

Spider stared back up at him, a touch of confusion lining his face.

"So, what, you brought the kid back with you?"

"Oh; no, I didn't."

"Why are you back here, then?"

Bear's smile fell into a straight, solemn expression and he puffed out a sigh.

"Well… when I saw what a nice home he'd been brought into and how relaxed he was in the company of the family… I felt kinda bad wanting to take that away from him. They had stuff there that we could never afford back in our old flat. He's starting school soon, he has a lot of catching up to do."

"So you're… leaving him there?"

"What else was I supposed to do?" Bear replied as he wiped his feet on the mat, letting himself in. Calmly, he slipped off his shoes and put them down neatly beside the door along with his bag, "I couldn't give him that sort of security. Even if we got a home, which isn't guaranteed, and I got a job that gave us enough income to live comfortably. My main concern has always been keeping him safe and… well, I just think he's safer with them more than he'd be with me. You know me, Spider," he added with a smile, "I'm hopeless out there on my own."

Spider strained a smile back at him, but was primarily still bewildered. He followed Bear up the stairs and into the kitchenette area, where Bear casually poured himself a glass of water.

"But Bear, all that work you put in, all that time and that long journey. You're saying that that was just… for nothing?"

"Not for nothing, Spider. I found my brother. I know he's safe. Hey, I can visit whenever I want. That wasn't a waste of time at all, I'm glad I can rest easy knowing Ambrose is okay. Thanks again for getting me there, by the way, I could never have done it without you."

"Oh- my pleasure," Spider stuttered, "I'm glad to have you back here, but… didn't you want to get outta this dump? The city, I mean. There's nothing for you here."

"I'm not staying. Not if I can help it."

"Oh?"

Bear nervously passed his glass from hand to hand, looking to struggle with what to say or how to phrase it. His gaze broke from Spider's eyes to instead absently focus on the scratched vinyl floor.

"You mentioned a little village a while ago. I've been thinking about it a lot. I was thinking… it would be nice to go and look for it," he finally managed to say.

At last, Spider gave a real smile of relief.

"An adventure! That'll be exciting. You sure you'll be alright on your own?"

"Well, that's just the thing," Bear continued, "I made a good friend recently, and it felt terrible leaving him after all he'd done for me… that's you, by the way, Spider. If you hadn't noticed."

A proud smile beamed on Spider's face at the thought of being a friend. A good one, at that.

"What I'm saying is, if you wouldn't mind putting up with me, I'd like it if you could come with me."

"I…" Spider started, taken-aback. Somehow, he hadn't expected to be part of anybody else's plans. He'd thought it'd just be him back out on his lonesome again after his little escapade, crawling around the city like the spider he was.

"I know I've been really inconsistent since you've known me. I keep going off on my own and then coming back. But you wouldn't have to worry about that, we'd be a team. Like… brothers. What do you say?" Bear asked him. Gingerly, he held out his hand, "You can say no."

Spider thought for a moment, but he knew really he'd been sold from the moment the idea was suggested. He reached out to shake Bear's hand the same way he'd done when they first met and closed his eyes with a content grin.

"Like brothers."

<u>Chapter 23: Ridicule in Hiddekel</u>

"I told you you were going to get yourself in trouble one of these days. But what did you do? You just kept going, huh?"

Leyland Mitchell crossed his arms and set his eyes on the concrete floor, seething in silence. Impatiently, he kicked his heel on the ground and drew his head into his shoulders like a disgruntled tortoise.

In front of him, through a layer of glass, sat an unimpressed nineteen year old with a white streak in his jet-black hair.

"After the whole accident, I didn't think anything could surprise me any more, but here we are," he continued, leaning back in his uncomfortable metal chair.

"I did what I had to do," Leyland replied in a low voice.

"*Poison* the dude?"

"He would have found out, Flye. It was just a precaution…"

"I can't believe you sometimes. There's a reason ma didn't want to come visit you."

"Why did you show up, then?"

"When I found out my big brother was in prison, I just had to come and see to make sure."

"That's low, man."

"Says the guy with the nine-year sentence."

"Whatever…"

Flye sat up straight at last and diverted his attention to the roll of toilet paper on the sill. He used a few squares of this to wipe his nose politely before continuing.

"So, where is he now?"

"Dunno'. Ran into him a few weeks ago and tried to talk to him but he didn't stick around."

"Shocker. Did he look well?"

"For a guy who drank bleach, yeah he did."

"Good."

Leyland paused for a while.

"Maybe you're right… I should have thought the whole situation through, but I panicked."

"Bit late for that now. But frankly I'm just glad you're finally realising that this obsession with your 'dead' childhood playmate is weird and unhealthy."

Leyland finally lifted his head to make eye contact. It was clear from the look on his face that he was realising the blue-grey uniform and sloppy 'food' wasn't his style.

"If you see Nico around… tell him I'm sorry," he said with a distinct tone of guilt.

Flye's face creased with scepticism.

"You think he'd forgive you just like that?"

"I don't know, man."

"Just a few weeks ago you were having a meltdown because you thought he'd try and kill you if he found out who you were."

"That was *different!*" Leyland snapped back. Seemingly surprised by his own volume, he immediately composed himself and sat back neatly in his chair. Sighing, he rubbed his palms, hoping that his short outburst wouldn't get him in trouble.

"I'll tell him. If I see him."

"I saw his girl a few weeks ago-"

"Nina."

"Yeah. She stopped and talked to me, said she still puts up posters sometimes. Missing person ones, you know? She's planning on moving soon if she can, to get a 'fresh start' or something."

"Did you not fancy telling her you knew where he was?"

Leyland shook his head.

Despite his confident and brash pretence, Flye knew that his brother could be a huge coward when his own reputation was at stake.

"Well," Flye started, casually rolling up his sleeve and checking his watch, "Looks like visiting time's over for us."

He got to his feet, chair scraping across the concrete floor as he did, and stuffed his tissue in his pocket. His brother looked back up at him with a gaze of dejection, sat there in his inmates vesture.

No doubt his nine year stay in Hiddekel Prison would drag on for what felt like longer than its actual duration.

"I'll be back in a month for the next visit," Flye continued, straightening his clothes and brushing down his jeans before he set his sights back on Leyland with a pondering stare, "...Or maybe I won't, who knows?" he shrugged. His relationship with his boisterous sibling had been rocky for as long as he could remember, and he found himself somewhat devoid of sympathy. Even growing up, Leyland had never been the greatest influence on him, but Flye had learned through watching the trouble Leyland got himself into over the years that it wasn't the best idea to follow in his footsteps. Looking at him behind the glass now, he only felt glad that he'd done better in his life.1

"Stay out of trouble in there if you know what's good for you."

"You know me."

"I'm serious, Leyland."

"I am too. See ya' later, kid."

"Yeah..."Flye grimaced at being addressed as 'kid', having just marked his nineteenth birthday, "See you." And he took his leave.

Even leaving the cold, hostile building, Flye felt a measure of relief. At least incarcerated, Leyland wouldn't be making any more life-altering bad decisions. Probably.

Hiddekel sat almost exactly central to the city. It was placed right on the border to the fenced-off 'danger zone', clearly to provide some dispiriting scenery to make life for the prisoners just that little bit more miserable. It was a dark, looming, redbrick building with a scruffy little car park where it was hard to find a space without a pile of rubble already occupying it. But if you wandered a little further down the street and made a few turns, you'd find yourself met with a wide, rented warehouse. Morris Krav Maga.

Flye had never met Marcus Morris personally, but he'd heard a lot about him. The fact that Leyland complained about the strict apartment rules told Flye he was a good person. He'd managed to keep Leyland mostly in check anyway.

As it happened, Marcus was on his lunch break, sat outside on a plastic chair with a Tupperware container of smoked herring and hardo bread in hand.

Flye hesitated, suddenly intimidated by the figure in front of him, who was easily six or more inches taller than he was, and twice as wide. But he pulled himself together and approached nonetheless.

"Hey, are you Marcus Morris by any chance?"

Marcus looked up with no change in expression.

"Sorry for interrupting your break," Flye added.

"No problem, kid. Can I help you?"

"Do you, by any chance, know a guy who goes by 'Spider'?"

"…I might. Are you one of his friends?"

"Yeah. He doesn't know it, though."

"That sounds about right."

"...Can you take a message?"